Penthouse Variations on

oral

erotic stories of going down

BY THE EDITORS OF
PENTHOUSE VARIATIONS

CLEiS
PRESS

Published in the United States by Cleis Press, Inc.,
2246 Sixth Street, Berkeley, California 94710.

Printed in the United States.
Cover design: Scott Idleman/Blink
Cover photograph: Terri Lee-Shield Photography/Getty Images
Text design: Frank Wiedemann

Certain materials herein were previously published in *Penthouse Variations* magazine.

PENTHOUSE, VARIATIONS, the PENTHOUSE VARIATIONS logo, and the One Key logo are trademarks of General Media Communications, Inc., and are used by permission.
First Edition.
10 9 8 7 6 5 4 3 2 1

Trade paper ISBN: 978-1-62778-093-3
E-book ISBN: 978-1-62778-099-5

Contents

Introduction

Seductive, mind-blowing, intense—those are just a few of the words that could be used to describe sublime oral sex. Whether giving or receiving, oral sex can be an intimate interlude or a lustful bacchanal. The seemingly simple act of pleasing a lover with lips and tongue is a heady aphrodisiac, a deeply personal moment when your arousal is completely interwoven with that of another. And that perfect mix of surrender and bliss is reflected in the tales in this collection, *Penthouse Variations on Oral*.

I can't think of a better selection of stories to launch the debut of this book series of erotica inspired by *Penthouse Variations* magazine. In its thirty-six-year history, *Penthouse Variations* has focused on the sensual confessions of devoted lovers who explore their lascivious fantasies—whether they're oral-only adventures, daring games of dominance and submission, or the carnal pleasures of turning duos into trios. But the one goal these men and women share is that they strive to make their thrilling dreams breathtaking realities—and lucky for us, they share every delicious detail.

Penthouse Variations on Oral serves up more than twenty tasty tales of oral delights. These sexy stories run the gamut from the unrestrained passion of brand-new lovers to the uninhibited exuberance of devoted couples. These people understand that oral sex isn't something to be rushed through or performed out of some sort of duty. Instead, it's an act to be savored, as arousing to the giver as it is to the receiver, which Adam Vane explains in his story "Secret Appetites":

I tricked my tongue in dainty circles all over her pussy, avoiding her pearl, but coming as close as I possibly could. I used my tongue and chin, and even my breath to warm her up. As I traced closer and closer, I felt her entire body trembling, and her reaction let me know that I was doing something right.... My cock throbbed fiercely in my khakis. This is what I'd asked for, and she was more than delivering, giving me a play-by-play of exactly what she wanted me to do. I'd never experienced anything sexier in my life.

On the flip side, Chloe Parker in "Screaming Orgasm" describes the joy of anticipation, knowing the skill of a familiar lover and letting past pleasures buoy her impending ecstasy:

Ryan knows how to please me. He starts off strong, then retreats, teasing and taunting, making me wait before coming at me once again with full force. By the time he's ready to fuck me, I've experienced several earth-shattering orgasms and my pussy is dripping with sex juices. I had a feeling this afternoon would be no different.

Penthouse Variations on Oral offers stories that are both entertaining and inspiring, giving you a taste of what can be if you release your inhibitions and indulge your appetite for passion.

Barbara Pizio
Executive Editor, *Penthouse Variations*

Lickety-Split

ALISON TYLER

Zach said, "I'll be there lickety-split," and I couldn't help myself. I started laughing.

"*What* did you just say?"

He was hanging up the phone, and he gave me a curious look, his ginger-colored eyebrows raised. "I told Jamie I'd be over in a minute." He ran one hand over his short hair in a habit I recognized from two months of working at his side.

"That's *not* what you said." Jamie was one of our regular clients. Her office always ordered a dozen coffees with various shades of cream and varieties of sweeteners. But for some reason Zach's response this particular morning had caught my attention. "You said *lickety-split*."

"It's just an expression," Zach insisted, helping to add the creams and sugars, label the paper cups and set the caps in place. He was working on autopilot, while I was trying to find a way to let him know that his casual remark had made my panties wet. I didn't rush, though. Zach and I had been flirting for months. We'd both started working at the café on the same day—neither one of us had seniority— and I was pretty sure that neither of us gave a fuck about management's no-dating policy.

Who was going to rat us out? We were there by ourselves.

Once he'd set the last lid in place, Zach hefted the box to carry it to Jamie's ad agency. I held the door open for him, and right as his well-muscled body was lined up with my own, I said, "When you get back, I have another type of split I'd like you to lick."

I thought he was going to drop the coffee. I could actually see the Rorschach-like splatter on the tiled floor in my mind—regular two sugars blending with decaf with soymilk—but he caught himself and said, "Back in two minutes. Hold that thought."

I held it. I held it as tightly as I possibly could, with my thighs squeezed together and my pussy positively clenched. Standing nearly frozen behind the counter, I willed myself to still my racing heart. As I exhaled, I looked at myself in the mirror over the fancy bronze coffee-maker. I had my blonde hair up in a French twist, every hair in place. The pink in my cheeks hadn't come from a cosmetic palette, but from my sexual excitement. Every sensual fantasy I'd ever had about Zach seemed to percolate in my head into one steamy concoction.

I took a deep breath and prayed for a slow day. Maybe we wouldn't have the normal commuters rush. Maybe we would be left to our own devices.

Maybes are worth about as much as a decaf soy latte in my

world. When Zach returned, I had a line of impatient customers that ran from the counter to the door, everyone craving their caffeine fix before a long day at work. Zach and I danced through our usual banter without a word about what I'd said until we'd served the last harried commuter. Only then did he sidle up to me, cradle my waist in his big hands and croon, "So, about this split?"

I grinned at him and took one of his hands in mine. Behind the counter, I slid his fingertips beneath the waistband of my short, checkered skirt and into my silky yellow panties. The expression on his face let me know when he felt the wetness meet him, envelop him, suck him in. After a few seconds, he withdrew his hand and slowly, oh so slowly, licked his fingers clean.

"How long have you wanted me to taste you?" His voice was hoarse. He looked as light-headed as I felt.

"Since that first latte."

"Excuse me?"

"Since the first day we were at work together. You made yourself a foamy latte, and you licked the rim of the cup before taking a sip. All I could think of was you licking my pussy in exactly the same way, with the same look of pleasure in your eyes. I'd never been jealous of a seventy-percent-recycled paper cup before."

"For two months you've wanted me to do this?" He slid his fingers back into my panties and used two of them to fuck me. I held onto the counter with both hands and stared straight forward. If a customer walked in, we'd probably be able to save face, although Zach might've had to work the cash register with sticky, pussy-scented fingers. But no customers interrupted us. Zach overlapped his two probing fingers and began to work me faster and harder, easily managing to locate my

G-spot. I'd never been so masterfully touched. My whole body felt electrified.

To my dismay, he pulled away before I could come, and this time, he spread my shiny gloss on my own lips. I was breathing hard. I stared into his eyes. He brought me to him, and with sweet finesse, he licked my lips clean. Then he kissed me. Really kissed me. Our tongues met, and I could taste my own honeyed flavor.

"How much do you want me between your legs?" he whispered when we parted.

"Desperately," I told him.

"Let's see how desperately," he said, and he went to his knees on the black spongy mat behind the counter and buried his head under my skirt. Okay, so now we were really walking the edge of decorum. I was still facing the door, ready to greet any customers who might enter the tiny shop. Zach had pulled my panties roughly to the side and was spearing my pussy with the tip of his tongue. He seemed to know instinctively how to touch me. At first, he tapped his tongue right on my clit. Then he started making circles all around. I recalled the way he created designs in the fancy coffees we served: leaves, stars and hearts. I believed he was tracing those same types of patterns with his tongue, as if I were a confection worth devouring.

What would happen if someone entered the store? I could take an order, and Zach would be hidden. But I wouldn't be able to move very easily to make the coffee. Not with Zach sealed to my pussy like that. The image made me giddy.

Luck was on our side for the moment. Nobody came in the store. Well, I'm lying. After a few more rotations of his knowledgeable tongue, someone *did* come in the store—and that someone was me. I shivered as a powerful climax worked through my entire body, from the tips of my toes all the way to the blonde tendrils creeping out of my French twist. Amazingly, I managed not to cry out, but only barely. I wanted to scream, to moan, to shout out Zach's name. *Oh, Zach! Oh, oh, oh, Zach!* But I didn't. I stayed entirely silent as Zach licked and sucked my throbbing clit, not releasing me until he could clearly tell that the vibrations had subsided. Only then did he pull out from under my skirt, wipe his mouth on the back of his hand, and stand up, smiling broadly.

Right at that moment, a customer entered the café. Still floating on the glittering endorphins of my recent orgasm, I served the stranger with such good spirits that he slipped a crisp five-dollar bill into the tip jar.

"Now it's your turn," I told Zach. I went to my knees before he could speak, but he pulled me right back up again. I was surprised. Didn't he want to feel my lips around his cock? Wasn't he as excited to sample the delights of my mouth as I had been to come on his lips?

"No—wait." He shook his head. "I don't want a quickie. I want to wait until we get off to...you know, get off."

I brushed my fingertips along the front of his jeans. He was dangerously hard. There was no way he could continue to serve people with a beautiful boner like that.

"*Can* you wait?" I asked.

"I've waited this long, haven't I? Two months of foreplay is the longest I've ever gone. A few more hours won't kill me."

It was clearly a dare. I didn't think he could manage the rest of the shift without release. However, Zach seemed determined to show me that I was wrong.

The morning went by ridiculously slowly. I taunted Zach whenever I slid past him, making sure to rub my butt against his erection. He smacked my ass and told me not to be cruel, but I was enjoying myself too much to stop. I created the foamiest latte I could, and I made sure to give myself a creamy mustache with every sip. Then I stared at Zach as I darted my pink tongue out to lick the foam away.

"You're bad," he said. "You're a cocktease."

"Not a tease. Not if you let me." I went on my knees again and pressed my face to the crotch of his jeans. He let me lick him through the denim and he sighed, but then he pulled me back up again.

"You'll have plenty of time to drain me after work," he said. "I'm not in this for a quick shot."

By the time the second shift arrived, Zach was nearly ripping through his pants. He grabbed my hand and pulled me to his car without a word, then began to drive me to his place. I had never wanted a cock in my mouth so badly before. I was actually salivating. In spite of him telling me to behave, I leaned over, undid his jeans and started to blow him on the drive. He let me, but he didn't come. I was more and more impressed with his stamina.

When we got to his apartment, Zach gave in. As soon as the door was shut behind us, he stripped and pushed me to my knees. I gave him head like a pro. I licked the tip of his cock, then slowly began to work my way down the shaft. I wondered how much teasing Zach could take. At the beginning, he simply leaned against the wall and let me work him at my own speed. I was interested to see if I could make him lose his cool. I mouthed the head of his cock and then began to suck on the knob. I indented my cheeks and really focused my attention on the first inch.

But after all that torture, Zach had reached his limits. He couldn't wait, and in a flash I understood why he hadn't wanted to go for it at work. Zach was unable to stay quiet. He gripped me and began to fuck my face, and as I sucked him, he moaned loudly. "Oh, baby," he groaned. "Your mouth is so warm. I can't believe this is happening. Finally. I've fantasized about this moment for so long."

He got louder and more explicit as I sucked him. I would never have guessed how dirty he was. He described the different images he'd jacked off to over the previous two months. "I wanted to have you suck me, and then jerk off all over your body. Then I thought about putting you up on the counter at work, spreading your legs and licking you to climax right there, where anyone could see." I rolled with the change of pace, flicking my tongue against the slit in the head of his cock before striving to deep-throat him. He never stopped talking, and I felt myself growing wetter at his words. He was turning us both on, and in seconds, I was drinking his cream, relishing every drop. He didn't stop talking even then, praising me for how I'd made him feel, telling me that heaven had nothing on my mouth.

"I had to get that out of the way," Zach said, "so I could take my time with you." We headed to his bedroom, where I stripped out of my clothes as fast as I could. We seemed to have the same idea. Sixty-nine was the number on both of our minds. Zach was on the bottom, and I climbed on top, and this time I got the chance to show off my oral expertise. I moved back and forth between bobbing on his rejuvenated dick and pushing forward so I could get in there and lick his balls. Zach spread me open with his hands and twirled his tongue around my clit.

"I wanted to eat you out that very first day," he said, when he came up for air.

"Yeah?" I was short of breath.

"You were wearing that little orange sundress, but it was so hot that day. You know, the first sweltering day of summer. The fabric stuck to you, and I wanted to peel it up and sink to my knees, wanted to see if you were wearing panties under the dress."

"And if I was?"

"If you were, I was going to eat you through them, suck on the front part until it was wet from you and wet from my mouth. Only when you were begging would I have pulled your panties down and given you the first feel of my tongue."

"And if I wasn't?"

"I didn't think you were. The panty lines would have shown, wouldn't they? So if you weren't, I was going to give you a spanking for being so naughty as to show up on the first day of work without knickers. And then I was going to eat your pussy until you came and then eat your asshole until you came again."

"Oh fuck," I sighed blissfully. "Oh god, Zach."

I had my lips around his cock once more, and I ground my cunt against his mouth, not so much to stop him from talking, but to get off on his words in a literal sense. It didn't really matter what he was saying now. He could have been reciting our special drinks: Shot in the Dark, Americano, Cappuccino, Black Eye, Black Tie, Zebra Mocha, Macchiato... The feel of those words against my most tender skin was what ultimately did me in. I came with an unexpected intensity, and my uncontrollable moans around his cock brought him to his own finish line. He climaxed a second after me, and I managed to drain him once more.

We were done in then, sprawled on the bed side by side, if

head to tail. Neither one of us had the energy to turn to be face-to-face. That was okay, though. I liked the view. On my side, I took the time to really gaze at Zach's gorgeous dick. He was a full eight inches, a powerful specimen. I had definitely lucked out in the cock lottery. With exploring fingers, I began to massage his dick. He started to do the same to my pussy, and I had the realization that maybe we weren't at the end of the road yet. I couldn't believe we were going to try for another round. But then, we had been flirting for so long. This was a situation that was months in the brewing.

I spit on my open hand and then began to work my palm up and down Zach's cock. He was coming to life again, growing harder by the second. He echoed my motions, touching me in the same rhythm. I began to breathe slowly and deeply, focusing as my pleasure built higher and higher.

When Zach had me on the very edge of climax, he moved us so that I was on my back and he was between my thighs. This robbed me of the ability to stroke his cock, but he told me not to worry. "Relax," he said, "we'll have all the time we need." I did as he instructed, lying back into the pillows and surrendering to the sensation of his tongue on my split. He alternated nipping and biting the tender skin of my inner thighs and licking my clit in broad, firm strokes. He even rubbed his short red hair against my skin, tickling me with the bristly fur of his crew cut.

"Oh Jesus, Zach," I whimpered.

"Put your feet up on my shoulders."

I did as he said, and he palmed my asscheeks in his hands and brought my pussy up to his mouth. He ate me as if I was a piece of fruit, but before I could come, he lifted me higher in his hands and started to rim my asshole. I had been hoping he might do that from the moment he'd confessed one of his fantasies, and I actually started to come the instant I felt his tongue probe my back door.

"Oh, the girl likes that," he said.

"Yes, Zach, yes."

He muffled his conversation with his mouth on my rosebud once more, and he licked and sucked my asshole until I thought I would see stars. When I was still in the throes of climax, he flipped me over and slid his cock inside me. How had I forgotten the pleasure of actually fucking? Up until this second, we'd relied on our fingers and tongues. Zach entered me with force, and he began pounding into me from the start. I buried my face in his pillows and cried out, loving every second of the ride.

"I'm going to shoot," he said, finding his voice again. "And then you're going to spin around and lick me clean. You'll taste me mixed with your own sweet juices."

My cries grew louder. Zach slid a hand underneath me to stroke my clit. How many times could a girl come in a day? I had no idea. I'd lost count. Zach fucked my snatch until I was caught in a series of unending climaxes—one after the other. I'd never had multiple orgasms before. But I thought I could definitely get used to the concept. On the wave of my contractions, Zach let loose and came inside me. My pussy continued to grip him and release him in a powerful inner embrace. When the vibrations slowed, he pulled out and spun me back around. I did as he'd described, licking the blend of our flavors off his dick.

He pulled me to him and held me in his arms in a sweetly sticky embrace. I felt completely demolished from the day's events, but then Zach said he was going to make us each an iced coffee for rejuvenation. "You know, with plenty of whipped cream on top and an extra shot of espresso for stamina."

"Sounds delicious," I told him, giving him bedroom eyes from the tangle of sheets.

"I think I'll even give it a name," he said as he walked toward the bedroom door.

We both smiled, and then said, "Lickety-Split," together.

Fine Dining

JUSTIN LEWIS

I've always said life is full of surprises—but so is my girlfriend, Sonia. A vivacious blonde with an upbeat personality and a hot body, she always finds little ways to thrill me, like getting us courtside seats for my favorite basketball team or leaving flirty notes in the last places I'd ever think to look. However, the thing that astonishes me most is her boundless creativity regarding oral sex.

One time, she called me at my office early in the day to invite me for a picnic. It was one of those unexpectedly warm fall days, and I liked the idea of getting out of the building for a while. However, I told her that I didn't think I'd have enough time during my lunch break to get to the park, eat and return. "Tell your boss you're sick," she insisted. "You're usually so responsible. I doubt he'll question you."

She was right, and what she had planned sounded better than going over spreadsheets like I'd been doing. From the huskiness of her voice, I had a feeling I'd be dealing with a different kind of spread, and I'm not talking about a blanket laid out with food. My cock grew hard at that thought, so I took a moment to calm myself before going to tell my supervisor I felt a migraine coming on.

I took the bus downtown and found Sonia waiting at the corner of the park where we'd planned to meet. She was checking her phone as I approached, but when she saw me, she ran over and threw her arms around my neck. Pressing my mouth to hers, I slid my tongue between her lips, and my dick stiffened again as we shared a long French kiss.

She broke away after a couple minutes of tongue sucking, grabbed my hand and led me down a path. The park was fairly empty because it was a weekday, and she brought me to a secluded spot surrounded by bushes and trees that was far from places where most people would congregate. In fact, the area was so perfect I got the sense she'd gone there earlier to scout out the location.

Sonia pulled a blanket out of her backpack, and we took off our shoes to weigh down the corners so they wouldn't fly up in the breeze. As soon as I sat, she straddled my lap and ground against me as we kissed once more. Though I wouldn't say the thought of food was more enticing than fucking my girlfriend, I wanted some answers, so I broke our kiss.

"What's for lunch?" I asked, realizing there wasn't much room in her small bag for the blanket *and* food.

She smiled mischievously and answered my question with one word: "Me." Now I grinned, at least until she attached her mouth to mine again, and then I lowered her to the blanket.

Pushing her shirt up over her tits, I tongued her nipples through her bra, but then I pushed that up to suck the rosy flesh directly. While I did that, Sonia reached between us and massaged my cock through my pants. It was clearly time to start making my way southward, so I kissed my way down her stomach until I reached the waistband of her jeans. When I looked up, she nodded enthusiastically, so I popped the button, pulled down the zipper and, after she'd raised her ass, pulled the jeans off, along with her drenched-through panties.

The scent of her lust was potent, and I breathed in deeply as I lowered my head to her moist center. She spread her legs wider as I got closer to her crotch and the petals of her pussy peeled back, revealing the ripe berry in the center. I was tempted to zero in on it, but I knew that would instantly trigger her orgasm instead of letting her build up to a bigger, and more pleasurable, climax. Instead, I sucked gently at her labia and ran my tongue teasingly over her slippery folds. I put my hands on Sonia's hips as she started writhing, and I lapped at her tender flesh, swallowing down my fill of her sweet-tasting juices.

Sonia threaded her fingers through my hair and grasped desperately at my scalp. She was trembling violently, and even though her thighs were clamped against my ears, I heard her gasps grow louder as I ate her cunt. She wasn't far from climax, so I tightened my grasp on her hips and pressed my tongue to her clit. That was all it took to make her cry out, and she continued announcing her pleasure as I drew small circles on her pulsating button. Then I slipped a finger into her and fucked her rhythmically, adding to her ecstasy. She howled so loudly I was afraid she'd alert passersby to our illicit activities.

To help her stay quiet, I moved one of my hands to her mouth, and she sucked my finger so ravenously that my dick twitched. I hoped that my cock was about to receive the same sort of treatment, and the thought made me slurp at my girlfriend's pussy even more passionately. She came again, and her body tensed as her pussy spasmed around my finger. We were both breathing heavily, and because my own need was so great, I raised my head from her still-quivering sex and moved up her body.

As soon as we were face-to-face, I kissed her. My lips were glossy with her juice, which she licked right off, obviously delighted by her own flavor. Her reaction to her taste on my lips turned me on even more, and I ground my cock against her to remind her that I was still eager for release.

"I haven't forgotten about you," she said as she reached down, undid my fly and pulled out my erection. Her hand was hot against my skin as she pumped my shaft a few times, as though to make sure I was good and ready—an act that was unnecessary. She quickly discovered the precome perched on the tip of my dick and massaged the fluid into my crown with her thumb until I was groaning with abandon.

I was going to come in her hand if she didn't change course soon, so while she continued working her fist over my prick, I muttered, "Please suck it," and kicked off my pants. She was immediately compliant, not even bothering to kiss or lick her way down my body as she pushed me back onto the blanket and headed straight for my manhood.

She started lower than I'd expected, laving my balls with long, slow swipes of her tongue before giving each a good, hard suck. My eyes were shut so tight I saw stars and my hands balled into fists, with a bit of the blanket trapped in each. My cock was impossibly hard and eager for her mouth's attention.

When she finally released my balls, she grasped my cock by the root. Swooping down, she wrapped her lips around my crown, and the heat from her mouth was intense in relation to the cool breeze that had been blowing against my skin. That sensation intensified as she worked her way down my length, swallowing me inch by inch until my pubic curls tickled her nose.

Moving slowly, she dragged her lips back up, keeping them tightly pursed so I'd feel the pressure, and tracing the underside of my shaft with her tongue. She maintained the lip-lock as she commenced blowing me in earnest, her head bobbing as her mouth moved up and down my length. All I had to do was lie there, let her do her thing and receive an insane amount of pleasure.

Of course, it couldn't last forever. My excitement kept skyrocketing, as she never wavered in her oral assault. My hips began pumping and my ass rose and fell on the blanket like I was trying to fuck her face, a motion I couldn't have stopped even if I had wanted to.

Not missing a beat, she moved right with me. Soon, my load rushed through my shaft. A second later, hot cream spewed from my crown and spilled out over my girlfriend's tongue. She gulped down each shot I fed her and kept sucking my prick until she'd drained me of every last drop.

When it was clear that my stores were empty, she released my cock and stretched out on top of me. We kissed, her mouth redolent of my semen, until I realized we were both still partially naked. Although no one had caught us in the act, I decided we shouldn't press our luck. Besides, now I was *actually* hungry, so we got dressed and then went in search of lunch.

That day in the park was thrilling, but it was nothing compared to the first time she'd surprised me with her sexual creativity. About six months into our relationship, Sonia invited me to accompany her to a wedding that was being held out of town, suggesting we take some extra days to have a real vacation. She made all the plans, including sending a car to drive me to what I thought would be the airport. However, I realized the driver was heading in the wrong direction. When I mentioned this, he said he'd been told to deliver me to the train station, and I had no choice but to trust him and wonder what Sonia had planned for us.

I found her waiting in front of the station when I arrived, two tickets in her hand. "I got us a sleeper car!" she exclaimed, and I remembered back to our first date, when I'd mentioned my fascination with the Orient Express, a conversation all but forgotten until now. Excited and intrigued, I followed her onto the train where we took our seats, my cock already at half-mast at the thought of the nighttime fun to be had.

Not that we made it till night. As soon as the train started moving, she leaned over and kissed me while stroking my upper thigh. I knew she couldn't miss the hard-on outlined against my jeans, and she responded by winking impishly and getting up to close the curtains. When she rejoined me, instead of sitting beside me, she knelt on the floor with her hands in my lap, working feverishly at my fly.

After fishing out my dick, she began to suck me right down her throat. I shut my eyes, leaned against the cushions and let out a deep groan as I put my hands on Sonia's bobbing head. For a moment, I was content to enjoy her tongue strokes, but then I decided that two could play at that game.

Pulling her onto my lap, I kissed her, sliding my tongue into her mouth as I hiked up her skirt and reached into her panties. Her pussy was already dripping, so I plunged my finger into her hole and stroked her from the inside as she pumped my prick in her fist. Then I pulled out of her, brought my finger to my mouth and sucked off her succulent juices. A second later, I remembered that our seat turned into a bed!

I slid her off me, and we quickly converted our seat before shucking off our clothes just as fast. Totally naked, we picked up where we'd left off, though, by an unspoken agreement, we were now positioned head to toe. Sonia was on top, and as she brought her cunt to my face, I touched my tongue to her slick petals. As soon as she was comfortable, she wrapped her lips around my cockhead and sucked like it was a lollipop.

As we settled into our sixty-nine, I heard people outside passing by on their way to the dining car, totally oblivious to what was going on inside our hideaway. I also felt the rhythm of the wheels racing over the tracks, and it didn't take long to figure out Sonia was matching her cadence to their revolutions. That was so sexy, especially with her honey pouring down my throat. The entire situation gave me a real taste of how amazing my new girlfriend was.

Her efforts inspired me to try to match her pace, but first I reached up and grasped her asscheeks to make sure she remained firmly in place no matter how the train might lurch. When I felt she was secure, I glued my mouth to her cunt and began working my tongue over her folds. At first, I flicked gently, but I soon increased the pressure of my strokes, occasionally grazing her clit.

Even though her entire body was trembling and she was gasping around my prick, she managed to do wicked things to me with her tongue. She'd rise to the top periodically and flick its tip into the slit in my crown to scoop up a droplet of precome. And whenever she did that, she cooed at the taste of my essence, sending vibrations down my shaft that reverberated all throughout my body.

Now she wasn't the only one gasping, although the sounds I made were muffled by her wet slit. We were caught in a circle of lust. With her breasts pressing to my body and her lips skimming over my cock, I felt her erect nipples poking against my torso. One of her hands was on my cock, and I lapped at her pussy with even greater hunger and nibbled her clit as my fingers massaged her ass.

Then I received my second surprise of that day. I was so caught up in what her mouth was doing—and bestowing a similar pleasure on her with mine—that I didn't notice the fingers of her free hand had crept between my asscheeks.

Before I was fully aware of what was happening, Sonia pressed the tip of a slickened finger against my asshole and massaged it gently. I hadn't noticed that she'd brought lube, but that's my girl—always prepared. Her actions felt great, and I relaxed, encouraging her entry. I wet my finger in my mouth before wrapping my lips around her throbbing button and reaching around her body to tease her tiny back hole at the same time.

As soon as I felt her slippery digit slip through my tight ring of muscle, I slid into hers while sucking her rigid nubbin. She sank in to her bottom knuckle before pulling out and thrusting back in, repeating that process over and over in order to fuck my asshole in the same rhythm as the swaying train and her unceasing mouth. I returned the favor by plunging in and out of her ass, causing her to moan blissfully. I couldn't get over the erotic intensity of doing this on a speeding train, and it wasn't long before I was rewarding Sonia with a mouthful of my cream.

At the moment I reached my climax, her thrusting digit was buried all the way to her palm. Thinking creatively as usual, she stroked me on the inside as my asshole spasmed around her digit.

Though she'd gulped my first volley of come, she only managed about half of the second, and the rest splashed against her breasts as she reached her own peak. I'd been announcing my orgasm by moaning against her pussy, and the vibrations, in tandem with my thrusting finger and my mouth on her extremely sensitive clit, finally sent her reeling.

Finding herself overstimulated, Sonia ripped her lips from my prick and threw back her head. She announced her arrival with a lusty cry, but I didn't shush her because the sounds of the train would most certainly drown her out. Instead, I concentrated on bringing her to another peak. I slurped at her pussy like there was no tomorrow, not stopping until my efforts paid off. She shouted my name as she came a second time, and then chanted "Justin!" over and over as she rode out her pleasure.

Although our berth was narrow, Sonia soon found a way to turn around and stretch out next me so that we could share a passionate kiss.

Tired from our orgasms, we let the train's rhythm rock us to sleep, though we awoke a few hours later for an encore. The train was a really exciting way to travel, and I know that trip set us on a path of fucking and sucking in unusual places, one that continues to this day.

Icing on the Cake

WILLIAM MCLOUGHLIN

Early on, it became pretty clear that my girlfriend, Ali, was into oral sex. But once I found out just how much, I considered myself the luckiest man on earth. I'd asked her to go bike riding early on a Saturday morning for what was to be our third date. Ali's extremely physical, so she was psyched about riding on the converted railroad trails near my house. Our goal was to do thirty miles that day. We are both personal trainers, so we're in good shape, but that was more than either of us had ever ridden in one day.

When I met Ali at six in the morning, she looked amazing in a black spandex top and bike shorts. Her long red hair was pulled into a braid that hung to the middle of her back. Immediately, my mind focused on how she looked naked, how tight she'd felt when we'd fucked. My cock swelled in my shorts.

Ali noticed my condition right away. "Maybe if you're good, I'll suck your cock behind a tree."

I almost lost it right there, and if she hadn't climbed on her bike and started down the street, I would have taken her in the middle of the road.

We rode for four hours, and I began to think Ali had forgotten her sexy promise. It made the time drag, even though it was a beautiful day. By then the sun was getting hot, so when we came to one of the small parks along the trail, it wasn't a moment too soon. We parked our bikes at a small snack bar, and Ali went to the window. "Do you want anything?" she asked over her shoulder.

I shook my head and drained my water bottle. Then I went to a water fountain and filled it again. When I turned around, Ali was sitting on top of a picnic table sucking on a cherry ice pop. I walked over and sat beside her, unable to tear my eyes away from her mouth on the frozen red stick. First, she licked up one side, then down the other. She did this a few times before flicking her tongue against the tip. Then she slid the whole thing in her mouth. Sweet juice dribbled down her chin, and she licked it away.

If that was how she sucked cock, I thought, I was in for the blow job of my life—that is, if she hadn't forgotten her promise. My dick was rock hard in my shorts as she continued licking, sucking and biting the frozen juice.

Ali must have noticed the look in my eye because she said, "I can tell you're having naughty thoughts." I smiled.

"But I have to warn you, this isn't how I suck a cock." She pressed the last frozen piece of the treat to my lips and smeared it around. "I enjoy sucking a cock much, much more. After all, an ice pop doesn't have balls to lick." She nipped my ear, then licked the stick clean of any remaining cherry juice.

She hopped off the table. "Ready?"

My cock was throbbing, and I was disappointed that she wasn't going to fulfill her promise right then and there. It was clear that she planned to make me wait.

I had to ride with an erection that did not seem to want to soften, especially since Ali was in front of me, her beautiful ass clearly visible rising from the seat. And my mind wouldn't let go of the image of her sucking that ice pop. It felt like an eternity before she pulled off to the side of the trail.

"Do you hear that?" she asked.

I listened for a moment and then shook my head.

"A waterfall," she said, and knocked down her kickstand.

I did the same and followed her off the trail onto a slightly worn path that led up a hill and into the woods. We walked for about a quarter of a mile before we came to a waterfall formed by the creek falling over an alcove. The sun shone through the trees and sparkled off the water.

"It's beautiful," Ali breathed.

I nodded and sat down on a rock, and Ali sat next to me. Her hand, resting on my thigh, began a light caress. She rested her head on my shoulder. "All I could think about this entire time was tasting you. I want you to fuck my mouth with your beautiful cock. I want to watch you come and taste your hot load."

The more she talked, the hotter I got, and when her hand came to rest on my cock, I thought I would explode right then and there. "Take your shorts off. Please," she whispered.

When I'd thrown my shorts to the side, she sucked in her breath and murmured, "Magnificent." Then she knelt on the ground in front of me and parted my legs by gently rubbing her hands up my inner thighs. But as much as I wanted her to touch my yearning cock, she didn't. Instead, she leaned forward and kissed my tender thighs while looking up at me. I could tell she was going to savor the experience.

My cock pulsed just inches from her face, and her warm breath tickled my shaft. Her tongue snaked out from between her lips and flicked at the sensitive head. Lifting my erection from its position against my stomach, Ali licked her lips as she passed her hand up and down the shaft. I shuddered, and she smiled up at me. "You're as hard as a rock," she said.

Placing my dick back against my stomach, she pushed my legs farther apart, then cupped my heavy balls in her hand. As she squeezed them gently, she watched my face.

"Fuck, that feels good," I said.

"Yeah?" she asked. "How about this?" She bent down and took one ball in her mouth and rolled it around with her tongue. I leaned my head back with a guttural moan. She rubbed me lightly with her hand as she paid the same incredible attention to my other ball.

From the delicious little sounds Ali made, I could tell that she was enjoying the experience as much as I was. Her tiny whimpers and moans vibrated against my sac as she sucked and rolled my balls in her mouth. My cock was ready to explode even though she was barely touching it. A drop of precome glistened on the tip.

When Ali noticed that, she left my balls and licked off the pearly fluid. "Mmm," she murmured. "Want to taste?"

I'd never tasted my own come before, but with that creamy

drop glistening on the tip of Ali's tongue, the experience suddenly seemed very appealing. I nodded, and she slid up between my legs to kiss me deeply. As our tongues danced, I savored the salty taste.

She smiled, sighed and licked her lips as she resumed her position between my legs. This time she took my cock into her mouth. She swirled her pointed little tongue around the sensitive tip, then pumped with her lips. My glans hit the back of her throat, and I moaned again. "Fuck, Ali. That's amazing."

She continued sucking me until my breathing became ragged and my balls began twitching again. Then she popped my cockhead out of her mouth and pushed my legs even farther apart.

"Do you know what my favorite part of cocksucking is?" she asked in an innocent little voice. I shook my head because I was speechless by that point.

"How hard a man's cock gets when I play with his tight little asshole."

I let out a groan at her words and looked down at her. An expression of intense concentration was on her face as she studied the area.

Then she looked up, caught my eye and made a great show of wetting her index finger with saliva. She continued staring into my eyes as she played at the tight opening with the tip of her finger.

"Ah...so tight," she whispered. Then slowly, she slid her finger in a few inches and my breath hissed out from between my clenched teeth.

"Do you like that?" Ali whispered. "Would you like me to fuck your ass?"

"Fuck, yeah," I breathed, and then gasped when she slid

another finger into my hole. The sensation was incredible, like nothing I'd ever felt before.

With her fingers still in my asshole, she leaned forward and took my cock back in her mouth. I knew I wouldn't be able to hold out for much longer. My balls were screaming for release.

Ali's pouty lips pumped up and down my shaft as she fucked my ass. I began to groan and rushed toward an impending orgasmic explosion. Then, as my moans became longer and louder and my balls clenched tightly, Ali replaced her mouth with her other hand.

Although I can't exactly say I was disappointed, I'd been looking forward to shooting my load down her throat. Then as my orgasm overtook me, she squeezed her hand at the base of my cock. And though it was one of the most powerful climaxes I'd ever had, she'd staved off my ejaculation. My whole body shook and I gasped, but the eruption I'd been expecting never came. I just sat there for a moment, amazed.

When my breathing had returned to normal, Ali smiled up at me. "Ready for the orgasm of your life?" she asked.

I thought I'd just had it, but I soon realized that I was ready to go again.

Ali's fingers had remained in my ass, and her mouth pumped up and down on my cock once again, seeming to relish my taste. It felt as if her lips and tongue were everywhere, nipping, biting, sucking me.

I felt the impending explosion once again, but this time she kept her mouth firmly around my shaft. I lifted my hips and stuffed my cock into her mouth, and she met me thrust for thrust. Finally, with one massive shudder and a loud, guttural groan, I shot my load into her mouth.

She sucked me dry as my whole body quaked, then laid her

head gently against my stomach until I had stilled and my breathing had returned to normal.

"Wow," I uttered. "When you said you'd suck my cock, you weren't kidding."

Ali proceeded to tell me how much she loved oral sex—the smooth feel of a hard shaft in her mouth, the way a man reacted. Nothing turned her on more. Hearing her words, my cock began to grow once again. I wondered if she enjoyed being on the receiving end of a tongue as much as she liked to be the one giving pleasure.

I pulled her up against me and placed her on the rock where I'd been sitting. Then I pulled those tight little bike shorts off as she braced herself and watched me. She spread her legs just enough to give me a hint of her delectable cunt, and I pushed her thighs even farther apart. Her musky smell greeted my nose, mingling with the fragrant summer air.

She watched me as I licked up one side of her slick lips and then down the other. As I moved closer to her clitoris, she quivered. But I didn't want to give her too much bliss too soon, so I played a while longer, tasting her moist vulva. By the tiny moans escaping Ali's pretty lips, I knew that she was enjoying every playful flick of my tongue.

Finally, I lapped her clit with the flat of my tongue and lashed it once with just the tip. A tremor wracked her sweet body, and letting out a long, low groan, she tossed her head back. "Oh yeah, just like that," she whispered hoarsely.

I repeated that pattern until her ass was wriggling on the rock and her hips were thrusting at my face. Then I made my tongue into a stiff point and stuffed it as far as I could into her pussy. She bucked even harder at that, and I added to my pattern—a slow lick over her clit, a flick of my tongue, then a long lick down to her cunt, where I thrust deep inside.

I must have done that for ten minutes while Ali's breathing quickened and her moans became more intense. Finally, she grabbed my hair in her hands. "I—I can't—" she began, then bit her bottom lip hard as I flicked her clit another time. "Please…please make me come," she managed to get out.

I shoved two fingers into her cunt just as she'd done to my asshole. "Oh, fuck," she ground out. "Yeah, fuck it."

I did exactly that, then I placed my face between her legs once again and began flicking her clit rapidly with my tongue. She let out a cry and her hips rose off the rock, thrusting against my fingers. I inserted a third finger into her slit and pounded into her with a steady rhythm.

By this time, her clit seemed to be swollen to the size of an acorn. I focused my attention on that heavy nub. She began crying out, trying to form words, but all that came out were distorted moans and ragged puffs of breath. Finally, with a series of screams and thrusts, her body shuddered and her cunt grasped my fingers as strong contractions ripped through her body.

I held Ali tight until she relaxed and her breathing returned to normal. Then I parted her legs again and took her clit between my lips. She seemed surprised, but she was soon moaning as I rolled the hard nub around on my tongue. Her body trembled from the intense pleasure as I sucked it like a nipple. Finally, I released her clit from the prison of my mouth and gave it a good tongue thrashing.

Ali began to moan as she'd done before, but this time, she bucked and thrust at my face for a good three minutes. Then her entire body tensed and lifted off the rock. Her mouth worked but made no sound, and her face was contorted in pleasure so intense it seemed almost painful. An enormous shudder wracked her body, and I could tell when the great wave of release flooded her. She spurted her sugary juice into my mouth, and I savored the flavor as she came back to earth.

Ali collapsed into my arms as I moved onto the rock and smiled down at her. "I see I'm not the only one who enjoys receiving oral sex."

She swallowed hard. "And I'm not the only one who enjoys giving it."

We spent the rest of the afternoon playing in the small water-fall, fucking and eating each other. Needless to say, we didn't reach our thirty-mile goal.

And, believe it or not, I still didn't know how much my sexy girlfriend enjoyed oral sex. That knowledge, however, came on our very next date.

A few days later, Ali called and invited me to spend the evening at her apartment. When she told me not to spoil my appetite before-hand, I assumed we would be going out for dinner.

Her apartment was beautiful—done in soft cream with a big fireplace at one end of the living room. She must have had the air condi-tioner going full blast, because it was freezing in the room even though a fire blazed in the hearth.

A sweet perfume assaulted me as she led me farther into her apartment. "It smells like a bakery in here," I commented. She smiled. "Do you like baked goods?" I nodded. Who doesn't?

She led me to a large bathroom complete with a two-person whirlpool bathtub, which was already filled with the jets running.

Ali stepped out of her clothes and into the tub, and I eagerly followed. Once we were both in the water, I kissed her deeply, ready to thrust into her cunt. But as I sucked on her nipple, she said, "You can play, but that's all for now."

I looked up, disappointed, and she patted my cheek. "You don't want to spoil your appetite, do you?"

It was the second time she'd said that, and I was beginning to think her warnings had nothing at all to do with food.

We still enjoyed soaping each other up and rinsing each other clean in the warm water. When we emerged from the bathroom, we were wrapped in fluffy white towels. Ali told me to lie on the blanket in front of the fire while she got something from the kitchen.

It was still freezing in her apartment, but it was nice in front of the blaze. I shed my towel and lay there naked, my cock still in immediate need of attention.

When Ali returned, her eyes were on my shaft. But my eyes were on the two fondue pots she was carrying. I asked what they were, and she just smiled. "Do you like chocolate?" she added. I nodded. "And do you like vanilla icing?"

Instead of answering, I tried to sit up to see what was in the pots, but she gently pushed me back on the blanket.

"Close your eyes," she said.

I obeyed, sensing I was in for a treat.

And I was right. It wasn't long before I felt a warm, thick liquid being poured onto my aroused cock. I looked down to find Ali coating me with chocolate—frosting my shaft like it was a cake.

She smiled at me. "Chocolate's my favorite." Then she urged me to lift my hips and poured the warm melted confection over my balls. That was enough to force a deep groan from my throat.

Ali began slowly, licking the excess chocolate off my thighs. Then she pushed my legs apart and worked on the rivulets that had trickled into my asscrack.

I'd never been licked there before, and my cock and balls ached in response. In fact, I was sure that if she kept it up, I could come without her ever touching my cock.

Eventually, she moved to my sensitive balls, sucking and rolling each one inside her mouth like some rare chocolate treat. At last, she made her way up my hard shaft. The chocolate had stiffened slightly, and she licked a straight clean path to my cockhead. A drop of pearly white precome mingled with the dark liquid perched on the tip, and Ali licked that off, too.

Then she took my whole shaft in her mouth. Her tongue was everywhere—licking, sucking and fucking me. There was no teasing now, just an amazingly sexy, chocolate-laced blow job, and I was in heaven.

I completely let myself go. I groaned and thrashed and fucked her until I came in her mouth. It seemed like an endless amount of come, but Ali drank it all as if it tasted just as good as the chocolate.

When I'd finished, she slid up my body, smearing herself with leftover chocolate and saliva along the way. She kissed me deeply, and I tasted the saltiness of my come along with the sweet confection.

Then I turned her on her back. Although my orgasm had been incredible, I was far from satisfied. I wanted this evening to last forever. I spooned the remainder of the chocolate out of the pot, blew on it, then dripped it over her tits. She gasped as the warm chocolate hit her nipples, but I wasn't done with her yet. I then reached for the pot of thin vanilla icing. I drizzled the warm, white liquid over her heaving breasts, and she trembled as if she were climaxing.

I licked the excess frosting off her skin before I concentrated on the hard tips. When I tongued her pointy nipples, Ali writhed in sheer pleasure. I licked and suckled until she was completely clean. She thrust her hips against my damp body the entire time.

While the sugary treats were tasty, I much preferred her own flavor. Rising up, I brought my mouth to hers, and we shared a lingering kiss. But before long, I sensed her hunger was too great. I worked my way downward, applied my entire mouth to her cunt and sucked. She ground against my face and wriggled her hips. "Please, more," she whispered.

I licked her swollen cunt lips slowly and carefully before devoting my attention to her clit. I bit it lightly, licked around it, then took it in my mouth like it was a piece of candy. I sucked and pulled and nipped until Ali raised her hips high, grabbed fistfuls of my hair and came with a shudder.

Sticky and sated, we collapsed in front of the fire. After a short rest—and a quick shower to wash away the remnants of our sugary fun—we spent the rest of the night fucking and eating each other... literally.

Tonight, Ali and I are scheduled to have our fifth date. She's promised something special, and my cock is already rock hard in anticipation of the sweet treat she undoubtedly has in store.

Face Time

MOLLY WEBSTER

"Screw Skype. Ignore your iPhone. BlackBerry be damned."

This is how the voice mail started. I stared at the machine, surprised by the intensity in my boyfriend's normally calm voice. Mike's from Massachusetts, but you don't catch a lot of his accent unless he's angry or excited. Now there was South Boston dripping all over my answering machine.

"Kick the Kindle to the curbside. Leave the laptop at home. What haven't I mentioned? Oh yeah. Bluetooth. Chew it up and spit it the fuck out. We are on our own this weekend."

I smiled and resumed packing. In his clever way, Mike was describing our much-needed vacation. We hadn't had a lot of time alone together lately. Our jobs required nearly 24/7 babysitting. There were weeks when we wouldn't see each other at all if not for some sort of 4G device. But it was difficult to fuck Mike when his face was reduced to a little one-inch box on the bottom of my laptop screen.

"We deserve a break," Mike continued, "and not a thirty-second break in between television shows. We need to talk to each other face-to-fucking-face."

The phone rang. I pressed the PAUSE button on the machine and glanced at the caller ID. Thank god, it wasn't the office. I lifted the receiver. "Hey, baby."

"You got my message?"

"Yeah, but what if people want to get ahold of us?"

"I don't want *anyone* to get ahold of you except me."

I smiled, but Mike didn't stop.

"In fact, what I really want to do is get ahold of your face and watch you part your gorgeous lips. And I want to know that you're not about to start talking into anything except *my* mic."

"Is that what you call him?" I teased.

"You know what I mean. How soon can you be ready?"

"Pick me up in five," I said as I zipped up my scarlet overnight bag.

"And I'm already here," he said. "Look out your front window."

Honestly, I understood why Mike wanted us to leave all of the electronic gizmos at home, but *this* was a prime example of why I appreciate modern technology. In the old days, pre-cell phone at least, Mike could never have called me up from the front seat of his vintage turquoise-and-white Chevy. I tossed my cell phone onto the bed and sprinted down the hall and out the front door.

"I thought you said 'no devices,'" I reminded him as I climbed into the car. He very purposefully pressed the OFF button and deposited the phone in the glove compartment.

"There," he said. "We're free."

I turned around and grabbed his overnight bag from the backseat. While Mike watched, I opened up the top and looked in, then put my hand in among his clothes and rifled around.

"Do I pass, officer?"

I nodded. He really *had* left everything at home. The only items in the bag were clothes and a toiletry kit.

"Face-to-face?" I asked, and then I bent over and began to kiss along the fly of his blue jeans.

"So to speak," he murmured as I began to work the zipper. We weren't even out of the city—we weren't even out of the driveway—and already I could feel my pussy pulse.

"More like fucking face?" I nuzzled his groin. I realized from the strength of his erection, waiting impatiently behind the wall of denim, that the mere thought of us without any way to be reached was a huge turn-on for Mike. Or maybe it was simply the fact that my lips were seconds away from closing in on his shaft. Suddenly, why didn't matter. Although we'd been talking about a romantic getaway, what I really wanted to get was the knob of his cock between my glossy red lips. Somehow Mike managed to engage the engine even while I started to rev his motor.

"That feels so good," he groaned as he began to maneuver the car down the street and toward the freeway entrance. I would have responded, but I was taught never to speak with my mouth full.

"Don't stop—whatever you do."

I sucked hard on the head of his cock and then began to bob

my head up and down on the shaft. I liked the thought that the drivers whizzing past us had no idea what was going on below my window. Well, nobody except any truckers who happened to cruise by, but I wasn't worried about that. Let them catch a thrill.

"Do you know how long it's been since we've been by ourselves?" Mike asked as I continued to work him. I shook my head. He groaned again. I knew he liked the movement on his cock. Just for fun, I pulled back a little bit, giving him a tease, but he drove his hips upward. He obviously didn't want to lose contact with the warm wetness of my mouth. Not to say that he was the only one enjoying this oral activity. Blowing Mike was turning me on, too. I could tell how wet I was without even slipping a hand between my legs to find out. I wondered whether he might consider pulling over for a rest stop. But how silly would that be? A rest stop ten miles from home.

"Touch yourself," Mike said suddenly. "I want you to play with your pussy while you suck me off."

I didn't have any trouble following that command. I let one hand drop to my lap so that my fingertips could circle my clit through my panties as I continued to lick and suck Mike's cock.

"Do you hear that?" Mike asked.

This time, I pulled off him slightly, and he shivered.

"Hear what?" I asked, before bobbing back on his cock.

"That sound…that sound of no cell phones, no beepers, no devices of any sort."

"There's a sound I *do* want to hear," I told him, letting his stiff cock slide free from my lips one more time. His entire rod was glistening and wet.

"What's that, baby?"

"The sound of you coming."

His hand found the back of my head again, and he pulled me down once more. I sucked him harder, understanding that he was getting close. This wasn't going to be a long, drawn-out exercise. We were simply setting the stage for our weekend away. It was, if you will, an *amuse-bouche*—something to excite the taste buds prior to the main event. That thought made me giggle, and the feel of my laughter around Mike's cock brought him to the edge.

He released the back of my hair, giving me the option to swallow or move away and watch the geyser of his come erupt. And although I *do* like seeing how much I turn him on, there was nothing that was going to stop me from swallowing his load.

I pressed my fingers deep into my pussy as I sucked him hard. I alternated between spiraling my tongue around the head of his cock and using the point of my tongue to drag a line down the shaft. I did all the naughty tricks I know he likes best, and then right when I felt him tense, I simply tightened around as much of his cock as I could hold in my mouth.

"Damn, Molly," he sighed, and I could feel his whole body shuddering. "God, baby, you do that so well." Mike groaned loudly as his shaft throbbed, and he released his first shot of come across my tongue. I swallowed each pulse greedily, and then I pulled off him, licking my lips and settling against the seat. I was almost there as well. But I was surprised when Mike reached for my hand and pulled it toward him. What was he doing? Oh, he was tasting my juices on the tips of my fingers. "So sweet," he sighed. "I can't wait to bury my face between your legs when we get to the hotel."

That image took me to the finish line. I used my moistened

fingers to pinch my clit, and I came in seconds—right there on the 405, in front of any weary fellow commuters who might have been watching. Mike observed as I readjusted my panties and pulled the hem of my dress down over my thighs. "You can try to make yourself look presentable," he said, "but I can't wait to let the slut out of the bag when we're by ourselves."

"This slut?" I asked.

"My one and only," he said with a grin.

I didn't think I could wait until we got to the hotel to get fucked. I was so wet and ready and hungry that the thought of a six-hour car ride to the getaway spot sounded more like hell than heaven. Sure, I'd just come. But something about this orgasm left me wanting more.

"Wait, Mike," I said, pointing out my window. "Look over there!"

"What? That hole in the wall?"

He was right. The spot looked like something you'd see in a horror movie. But right now, the motel could have been the Taj Mahal, or possibly Hotel California. I didn't care whether they had pink champagne on ice or not.

"Please, pull over."

"Everything okay?" he sounded concerned.

"I want more…more than you can do to me in a car."

"But Molly," he started, "you won't believe the spot I chose for us. The shower is open to the ocean. From the room, you can hear the waves lapping."

"Lapping," I insisted. "That's what I want. I want your face between my thighs, your tongue on my clit. Lapping. Come on, Mike.

Please." The yearning inside of me was growing by the second. I put my hand on his arm. "Please."

I could tell he was acting against his better judgment, but I watched gratefully as my beau signaled and exited the freeway. We'd probably driven by this lonely motel hundreds of times on our way from L.A. to San Francisco without ever noticing. That was the kind of spot this was. Yet as we pulled in, I saw that the place wasn't the Bates Motel. This was much more like a spot that had almost been untouched by the passing years. The Spanish-style bungalows were quaint and pale pink—nearly matching the mountains. Even better, there was not a single wi-fi sign anywhere to be seen.

Mike wanted us to be unreachable. *This* was the perfect spot.

"Are you sure?" he asked as he pulled into a parking spot. "Because I've seen pictures of the room I booked. I looked at all the choices online and picked the very best one. I mean, outside you can see this gorgeous rocky outcrop, the glitter of the waves, the sunspots on the ocean, golden circles that look like magic."

"Golden circles," I repeated, nodding. "Everything you're saying makes me hornier. I want to make circles around the head of your cock and draw you into my mouth again, baby. I *can't* wait."

Mike was sold. He walked into the office and came back in moments with a key ring dangling from his fingertips. I had to laugh. The number on the key fob was *sixty-nine*.

"We'll stay here for a few hours," he said as he held the car door for me, "and then I'm taking you north."

"But right now," I said, grabbing his hand and hurrying to the room. "I want your mouth—south."

He was as excited as I was when he unlocked the bungalow.

We didn't even bother to look around at the digs. We were stripping off our clothes, hurrying for the bed. Why had we even needed to leave the apartment if all we were going to do was go topsy-turvy? Because at home something is always beeping. *Someone* is always calling. The only thing making noise now was the sound of my heart in my ears. Mike picked me up and threw me on the mattress.

He didn't ask me what I wanted. He didn't dally at all. He practically dove into my pussy headfirst, his hands spreading apart my nether lips, his tongue strumming against my clit. I swam in the sensation for a moment, simply letting the pleasure take over, but then, oh damn, I needed something to suck on.

I couldn't lie there and take it. I needed my hands on Mike's skin, my mouth on his cock. The taste I'd gotten in the car had only whetted my appetite.

But before I knew what was happening, Mike had pulled away.

"What are you doing?"

"I want you to taste how sweet you are," he murmured. In moments, he was fucking me, his hard, throbbing cock thrusting deep into my pussy. And then, just as quickly, he had pulled back again, slid us into that crazy sixty-nine and was letting me lick my own juices off his shaft. I was dizzy with lust from the motions—so turned on by how he was running our show.

Mike always says I taste like nectar. Ambrosia. The most delicious honey he's ever imbibed. Now, I could see what he meant. But I couldn't see for long.

"What—wait!"

No, he was moving once more, this time positioning me

doggie-style and thrusting his cock quickly in and out of my pussy. I was lost. I wanted to keep sucking him. And I wanted him to continue to play those amazing games with his tongue around my clit. But I also wanted to be filled like this—to be fucked like this. Yeah, Mike always says it. I'm a greedy little slut.

"What do you want?" he asked, taunting me.

But two can play that game.

I squeezed him with the muscles of my pussy. He started to breathe a little more heavily. "What do I want?" I asked, and I spoke in my sexiest whisper. "I want to lick your cock from shaft to tip."

He groaned and fucked me harder.

"And then I want to lick your balls, gently. Just the way you like."

"Oh, fucking hell."

"And then," I said, "I want to grind my pussy against your face so that I get off exactly when you get off. How does that sound to you?"

He didn't answer with words. Instead, he pulled off me again, and I scrambled around so that I was beneath him. So sweetly, so softly, I licked his balls, exactly as I had said I would. Then I moved again so I could work my tongue up and down his shaft. Mike let me play with him for a moment—feeling the same way I had earlier. There is that moment when the pleasure is almost overwhelming, when the feeling of having warm wetness caressing your private parts can take your breath away. But in seconds, he recovered and began to reward me.

I tongued his cockhead; he suckled my clit. I licked around the head; he treated my clitoris as if it were a piece of hard candy—his favorite flavor. Then he upped the energy and the intensity. Without really moving his mouth from my pussy, he started to talk to me.

"What you did to me in the car was so naughty."

I moaned.

"You knew that, too. You knew exactly what you were doing. I'll bet you planned all of it from the moment we decided to take this trip."

I chuckled around his cockhead. He was right. I'd been wanting to set the mood for our vacation from the very first moment his foot hit the pedal.

"But it's unfair," he said. "Because I couldn't return the favor."

I tried to imagine that. Yeah. Sixty-nining on the 405 would have been mighty difficult. "But someday we'll get a limo," he said, "and we'll do it in traffic."

That sounded good to me, but I couldn't respond. I was consumed with his cock, moving my mouth up and down. Mike ran his fingers through my curls, cradling me as I blew him.

"Fuck, you're so delicious."

The words rumbled through me. I could understand him, mostly, but it was both what he said and how he spoke the words that made me tremble all over. "I can tell when you're getting closer to coming," he told me. "You get even wetter." When he was speaking, he brought his fingers into the action, spreading my lips apart, holding me open.

I sighed.

"Let me make you come."

"Yessss," I slurred around his cock.

"And then let me come in you."

I nodded as well as I could since my mouth was still filled

with his rod. Mike began to really work me. He licked and sucked. He tricked his tongue in devious circles around my clit. He applied just the right amount of pressure to just the right spots. And then he gripped my clit between his lips and simply sucked in a wavelike rhythm. Suck. Release. Suck. Release. Suck. Release. Until I was coming. He felt the shift in me, and he immediately let go of me with his mouth and moved my body once more.

Feeling his cock slide into me while I was coming was almost more than I could take. My pussy was still contracting—tight, tight, *tight*—and he gave me something thick and hard to hold on to. I started crying because it felt so good. I couldn't remember the last time we'd given ourselves so deeply to each other. It felt as if he'd stretched out my climax into a million orgasms. I came and came, grinding my hips against his body, holding onto one of those flimsy pillows, trying not to scream, but then failing.

"Ah, sweet baby girl," Mike moaned as he came. He lifted me off the bed with the power of his thrusts, and then he settled down against me, so that we were cradled together, sweaty and satisfied.

"Let's shower here," he said, "then try to make it up the coast without another stop."

"We're going to shower?" I asked, dirty thoughts already filling my head. Mike had promised me a weekend filled with face-to-face communication. But he wouldn't mind taking me from behind against the tiles, would he?

Hungry for More

BRIAN GARDNER

Cunnilingus. Such a beautiful word. *Lingus* is Latin for tongue, and we can all guess what the *cunni* means. I can think of no other activity I would rather be doing, no other place I'd rather be, than between the soft, silky thighs of a beautiful woman, swabbing my tongue up, down and around her wet, pink pussy. Pussy, another mellifluous word. Just like labia, vulva and clitoris. They could be names out of Tolkien, but instead they are the most tantalizing parts of a woman's body, parts that I long to taste.

There seems to be a mystique about eating pussy, and I suppose something that marvelous would shroud itself in mystery. Guys who can do it well attain a sort of status that only ninja warriors seem to attain. And though there are many colorful euphemisms to describe it, the simplest phrase describes it the best: eating pussy.

Over the years, I have become somewhat of an expert at this, if I can be immodest. But I certainly didn't come by this knowledge instinctively—I had to be taught. For that, I owe my college girlfriend, Rhonda.

Rhonda opened my eyes to many things. She was a genuine free spirit, and I learned about art, politics and philosophy from her. More important, she taught me the art of performing perfect cunnilingus.

Thinking about her now gives me a warm glow of nostalgia, as well as a lump in my pants. We met in a film class, and I was immediately smitten with her big blue eyes, button nose and dimpled cheeks. She wore her brown hair in a boyish cut that accentuated her cute face.

My relationship with Rhonda lasted for a few years, and during that time we had many memorable sexual encounters, but one of our first times together really stands out in my memory. It was a Saturday afternoon in the spring, and a pouring rain drummed against the roof of Rhonda's house, canceling our plans for a picnic. Instead, she lit a few dozen candles, put a jazz CD on the stereo and invited me to take a bubble bath with her.

I had wanted to suggest that we just hop right into bed, but something in her voice told me that following her lead would end up being worth my while. In fact, as we slipped into the hot, soapy water, Rhonda gleefully informed me that she was taking charge, and if I listened to her all afternoon, what would follow would "blow my mind." I eagerly agreed, especially when her lathered hands reached for my stiffening cock.

We washed each other thoroughly, and after we climbed out of the tub and dried each other off, she led me by the hand to her bed. We stretched out on the mattress and she told me she wanted me to use my tongue and hands all over her body, going as slowly as I possibly could. Then she looked up at me expectantly, her eyes glistening in the candlelight. Tentatively, I ran my fingers across Rhonda's arm. Her skin was so soft that I shuddered with anticipation. She shivered also, and bade me to continue. My fingers danced across her flesh, and her nipples visibly hardened. When I tweaked them, she cooed and told me to suck them. I bent forward slowly, knowing instinctively not to rush things and pop them in my mouth like grapes, though that was what I wanted to do. Instead, I began by lightly kissing along her cleavage and then slowly around the curve of her breast, spiraling inward toward her nipple. She moaned softly and ran her fingers through my hair. Eventually, I took a plump nipple into my mouth and sucked it gently. Rhonda told me to flick my tongue against it, and I did so, which made her body squirm beneath me.

When I'd had my fill of her cherry-red nipples, I busied myself with the rest of her flesh. I kissed her neck, ears, shoulders and stomach, careful not to miss an inch. My cock was extremely hard, but I resisted the urge to touch myself and focused only on Rhonda. She rolled over onto her stomach, and I peppered her back with soft kisses all the way down to her sweet little ass, which I caressed with my tongue.

I methodically made my way down her legs. She kept up a patter of murmured encouragements, but clearly I had caught on quickly and didn't need much instruction. When I got to her tiny feet, I really turned her on by sucking on her toes and licking her soles.

The CD had been set to repeat mode and was making its third

go-round by the time Rhonda rolled back over. Her eyes were absolutely glazed with lust, and she spread her legs, showing me the glistening wetness of her shaved pussy. My mouth watered as I gazed down at the delectable sight between her thighs. As I began to lean forward, she put her foot on my chest and said, "Take it slow. Ease into it."

Nodding, I put my lips on her ankle, and then began kissing my way up her calves. The smell of her arousal, mixed with the aroma of the candles, was so heady I almost swooned. I got closer and closer to her pussy and circled it with my tongue. Her labia puckered, and I let a puff of breath waft across them. Like a butterfly, I let my tongue land softly on her moist slit. Ever so slowly, I began to kiss and lick her pussy, and her lips opened like a blooming rose.

Now Rhonda put her hands on my head to guide me. She instructed me not to attack her clitoris directly, at least not yet. I saw it clearly, poking out from its hood, and resisted the temptation to suck on it. Instead, I continued to lick up and down her slit. Following her directions, I got my fingers into the act, inserting two inside her cunt while pressing my thumb against her mons. Once I began sliding them in and out, she told me to go ahead and run my tongue against her clit.

When I did that, Rhonda shouted and nearly threw me off the bed. I decided to go for broke and began buzz-sawing her clit as I finger-fucked her. The pitter-pat of the raindrops against the roof punctuated my ministrations perfectly, and in just a few minutes she flooded my mouth with her nectar. She mashed her sex against my chin, and the walls of her vagina clamped around my fingers. I held her tightly, continuing to eat her pussy even as she shook through her orgasm.

When Rhonda recovered she snuggled against me, my hard-on

pressed firmly against her soft thigh. After a few minutes she looked up into my eyes and said, "Now that's how you eat pussy."

I was rewarded moments later. Starting at my ear, she gave me a thorough tongue bath, spending most of her time and concentration on licking my cock and balls. With a talent I never knew she possessed, she would bring me to the edge of an explosion before she'd back off, squeezing my prick in her hands. Then she'd start again, either sucking my balls into her mouth or licking up and down my shaft. I was almost delirious before she finally began sucking me in earnest, bobbing her head up and down over my entire length while fondling my balls with her fingers. She had a hungry look in her eye that told me she was ready for my come, so I let go and filled her mouth with my frothy cream. Rhonda swallowed it all, except for a bit that trickled out of the corner of her mouth. Then she sat astride me, smiling beatifically, and slurped that up as well.

Before that day was over, Rhonda had given me a few more lessons in the art of oral sex. That was when I realized I had a predilection—and a talent—for cunnilingus. I became addicted to going down on her, and I was disappointed when we got jobs in different cities and went our separate ways.

Rhonda, however, had taught me well, and there have been a number of women since who have been the recipients of the knowledge she imparted. My most recent girlfriend, Abby, has even asked me to say thank you for her, if I ever get the chance.

Abby started working in my office about a year after I did. Confident, she strode around the office in her smart corporate suits, her long, red hair flowing down her back. I was instantly smitten. Fortunately, the attraction was mutual, and we began to date. She was a little sexually inexperienced, though, and wanted to take things slowly. I liked her enough to wait until she was ready, but I couldn't help fantasizing about the first time I'd go down on her, and what her pussy would taste like.

After a few months, Abby and I decided to spend the weekend at a bed-and-breakfast in the mountains. We drove there after work on Friday and got to the inn at close to midnight, too tired to do anything but unpack and go straight to bed. It was the first time we would be spending the night together, though, and I was wondering exactly what was going to happen.

Abby went into the bathroom and closed the door. I waited expectantly, and when she emerged she was wearing an ankle-length flannel nightgown. She looked quite radiant in it, but a tad too wholesome for my taste. I had been hoping for something a bit more risqué.

We climbed into bed, and she nestled against me. I held her, but we were both so tired that it was only a couple of minutes until we fell asleep.

The next day we skated almost all afternoon on the pond next to the inn. I hadn't skated since I was a kid, and she ran rings around me. After falling for about the twentieth time, I took a seat on a bench and watched her glide across the ice. She had a whale of a time, and her pink-flushed cheeks made her look almost unbearably sexy. I hoped she wouldn't tire herself out so that we could have some fun later that night.

Afterward, we enjoyed a fine dinner at the inn and then went upstairs to our room. I suggested we take a bath together. Abby seemed a bit uncertain, but agreed. We went into the bathroom and slowly undressed each other as the tub filled with water. She had a slight yet athletic build, with lovely small breasts capped by pink nipples. She stood before me, shyly crossing her hands in front of her crotch, which was framed by a tuft of strawberry-blonde hair. Then she took a good look at me and blushed because my cock, in anticipation of what was to come, had filled out and was hard and pointing right at her.

I took her hand, and we slipped into the water. Abby sat between my legs, facing away from me. After I scrubbed her back, I reached around to cup her tits. She moaned and leaned back against me, squirming against my cock. My soapy hands found her pussy and rubbed it, my fingers dancing between her folds. She held her breath as I caressed her, but I broke off contact before she neared orgasm.

Stepping out of the bath, we toweled each other off and headed back to the bedroom. Then I turned the bedside lamp on its lowest setting and put a silky scarf of hers over it. The room was now enveloped in an amber glow, the perfect complement to her peaches-and-cream complexion. I then suggested that she lie on her stomach on top of the covers, and she complied.

I ran my fingers lightly across her back, ass and thighs. I wanted to get close to her pussy, to taste it, and knowing I would be the first to do that made me giddy with excitement. Abby trembled as I touched her and pulled up her knees so that they were tucked up underneath her body. With her head buried in the pillow, it was a very erotic pose. Her ass, which was firm and smooth, glowed in the lamplight. I salivated as I moved in to kiss it.

Abby squealed as I trailed my lips over her ass. Then I pulled apart her cheeks slightly and swiped my tongue across her succulent rosebud a few times, making her jump a little. Finally, I lifted her hips slightly to get at the main course. Her labia were puffed and the same pink as her nipples, with just the slightest amount of dew on them. I touched my fingers to the moisture, gently spreading it around, lubricating her. She continued to squeal into the pillow as I massaged her nether lips between my fingers. More dew seeped from within, until she was soaked.

Sensing that now was the time, I moved my mouth to within millimeters of her cunt. I let my breath fall on her slickened mound, which made her shudder. Then I ran my tongue across her pussy and she yelped. I backed off for a moment, letting her know that she was in control of the pace, and she was quiet. Then she hungrily whispered the word I had hoped to hear: "More." I smiled and went back to work.

With increasing intensity, I continued to lick and suck on just her outer labia. The continuous flow of juice told me I was on the right track, as did the moans and groans that increased in volume. Taking it to the next step, I reached in and parted her lips, and as the petals were spread, I got a good look at what lay within. Hungrily, I lapped at her opening, thrusting my tongue as deep as it would go.

Soon I started getting a little stiff from the position I was in, so I urged Abby to turn over onto her back. She looked so beautiful, her face positively beaming. I kissed her thighs and spread her legs wide, then dove into her pussy. Her lips were fully apart, and I rubbed my face between them. Then I found her clitoris with my tongue, which made Abby yelp again. I licked all around it, only occasionally returning to directly make contact with that little nub.

I sensed Abby was ready to come, and that it would only take a little push from me to make it happen. I inserted two fingers into her very tight pussy and began finger-fucking her as I licked all around her clitoris. When I felt her cunt walls clamp down on my fingers, I attached my lips to her clit and sucked. That did it. She pressed her legs tightly against my ears, bucked her hips and came in my mouth.

It took her several minutes to come back to earth. I held her tightly as she shivered, feeling kind of proud of myself, and then I felt her fingers snake around my cock.

"I've never sucked a cock before," she said softly, stroking me up and down. I told her there was a first time for everything, and that there was no such thing as a bad blow job. She giggled and shifted her body so that her head was right between my legs.

I gave her some hints as to what I liked, which she happily complied with. She licked my balls and the base of my cock, then took the head in her mouth and swirled her tongue around it. This made my body jerk, and Abby looked alarmed. I assured her that it felt great and told her to keep going. She did, taking my entire head into her mouth, sucking and circling it with her tongue. She was a natural, and when I told her so she smiled and got more aggressive.

Eventually, Abby took about three-quarters of my shaft into her mouth and pistoned her head up and down as she fondled my balls. She said she loved the taste of my precome, and now that I had introduced her to oral sex, I would have a hard time stopping her from doing it all the time. That sounded great to me!

It wasn't long before I was nearing my climax, so I asked her if she wanted to swallow my come, or if I should withdraw. She thought this over for a second and then said she was game, and resumed sucking my cock. A few seconds later, I filled her mouth with cream. She swallowed most of it, though a few drops still coated her lips. To my delight, she licked those off like she'd been sucking cock all her life.

The rest of that weekend was one of incredible discovery. Most of it was of the oral variety, as Abby learned that not only did she love to suck cock, she happened to be very good at it. She also loved to have my tongue wiggling in her cunt, bringing her to climax after climax. We never made it back out onto the ice, and we hardly broke for meals. We were too busy eating each other! Our shared love of oral sex continues to this very day, as the lessons Rhonda taught me have served us both well.

An Erotic Feast

Maria King

"Try this, Maria," Raymond said, smiling and offering me a bite of decadent pasta. Obediently, I opened my mouth and let him feed me, then I slowly licked the rich, buttery sauce from my lips, savoring every delicious drop. As always, a dish from Raymond's kitchen thrilled the senses.

"Spectacular, right?" he crooned, reaching out to stroke a honey-blonde wisp of hair away from my eyes.

I nodded enthusiastically. I might be a tad biased, but it seemed I wasn't the only one of that opinion. That night, we'd offered an all-you-can-eat special at our restaurant. Every bit of food had disappeared—all except for the small plate of pasta Raymond had saved for me.

"When you finish that, there's much more waiting—"

I looked at him quizzically. I'd seen the kitchen. We'd been completely cleaned out. "What do you have in mind, Ray?" I asked, my blue eyes narrowing.

"Chef's choice," Raymond said. "Put your appetite in my hands."

Curiosity piqued, I agreed. Immediately, Raymond cleared away the dish, then lifted me up and spread me out on our largest wooden table in the center of the restaurant. I continued to gaze at him, taking in his auburn goatee and his sharply featured face, marveling at the way he managed to look so dashing, even in his chef's whites.

Gently, Raymond ran his strong hands along my stocking-clad legs, sending instant tremors through me. "I thought you might enjoy a little all-you-can-eat fiesta of your own." He paused. "Or, rather, an all-we-can-eat treat."

His words—and his voracious expression—let me know precisely what he was in the mood for. I knew that he was going to dine between my thighs, and that I was in store for the best pussy-licking in the world. Raymond understands how to use his tongue, and I was quivering with anticipation. "You're the one who's hungry now, aren't you?" I asked.

"Ravenous."

"So what are you waiting for, baby?"

"Every good feast deserves to be savored." He grinned, already in motion as he spoke, reaching underneath my skirt and sliding his warm fingertips against my panty-clad pussy. My juices had managed to seep through my peach-colored satin undies. I'd gotten wet quickly, and I knew this was partly due to the thought of fucking in our restaurant.

In the past, we'd never taken our sex sessions further than heavy-petting marathons in the kitchen. But with the front door locked and the lights on dim, it was the perfect moment for an amorous adventure.

Raymond believes that a good meal deserves his total attention. To my great delight, he feels the same way about fucking. He never skips any important steps in the preparation. He says that I'm like a wonderful dish that requires constant attention in order to achieve the desired effect. And that night was no different. With a purposeful look on his face, Raymond stood directly in front of me and pulled me toward him. Leaving my stockings on, he bent down and kissed me, working his way up my thighs to the hem of my skirt. When he reached the split of my body, he pressed his face against the skirt and licked and kissed me through the silky material. I felt the wetness and the heat through my clothing, and it turned me on dramatically.

I moaned as he continued to rub his face against me, and then I made more urgent noises to let him know that I was desperate for him to explore beneath my clothing. Every rotation of his face against my pussy brought me up one notch higher on the pleasure scale. My impending orgasm was going to be fierce. As he pressed more firmly against me, my moans grew even louder. Finally, Raymond brought one hand under my skirt, and his fingers tapped a sexy code against my satin-covered pussy.

"Take my panties off," I begged. "Take everything off."

"Everything?" He was teasing me, hoping I'd spell out each spicy detail.

"If you don't, I will," I threatened.

Apparently, that's what he'd wanted the whole time. "Then do it," he teased. "Strip for me, Maria."

Charged by the look of desire in my husband's shining eyes, I stood up on the sturdy wooden table and provided him with a sexy striptease. First, my black mules came off, kicked clear to the corner of the room. Next, I unzipped the short black skirt and let it fall past the subtle curves of my hips. With a nudge of my toe, the garment disappeared over the edge of the table. I was getting more and more into the moment, enjoying every shimmy of my performance.

Slowly, I peeled down my inky-black nylons. I could see myself in the oval-shaped mirror hanging behind the bar, and I knew I looked good. My heavy spill of deep-blonde hair shimmered past my shoulders. My well-toned legs looked enticingly long as they disappeared under the hem of my crisp white top, which was still buttoned primly to the collar. With one firm tug, I had the whole row of buttons undone. I tossed the shirt away and then removed my bra, winging it overhead the way a real stripper might do.

With Raymond so clearly fascinated by my every move, I wriggled out of my panties and let them drop to the table's edge. He quickly snatched up the discarded garment and brought it to his face. I felt a shiver snap through me as I watched my husband breathe in the darkly seductive scent of my arousal, which was lingering on my panties.

"Down," he hissed after inhaling the aroma. "Get down on the table, now."

I waited one beat longer, just to taunt him, but Raymond had tapped his reserve of patience.

"Lie down again, sweetheart. Please. I'm so hungry."

"Good," I cooed, as I obliged his request. I was enjoying Raymond's game now. "We have a special available tonight: an all-you-can-eat smorgasbord."

I hadn't even finished speaking before Raymond's face was between my legs, his hands cupping my ass and effortlessly lifting me up to his greedy mouth. In a second, I felt his whiskers tickling my naked skin and then his tongue parting my pussy lips, searching out the treasure of my swollen clit within.

Raymond paused and then breathed lightly against my tender skin, letting me stew in my own juices for several seconds until my own breathing started to speed up and my fists clenched and unclenched uselessly at my sides. Next, he pinched my lips open using just the right level of strength, holding onto me firmly even though I was so slippery wet. I was at the point of screaming with need when he finally let me feel his tongue, once or twice, in gentle, caressing strokes. He was careful to not go too hard or too soft. Then he massaged my pussy thoroughly with his whole mouth, not leaving any area wanting. He understands that I ultimately require a more focused touch to achieve climax, but at the beginning I'm more than satisfied to be treated to a full realm of sensations, and he's happy to deliver them.

As I grew more turned on, Raymond traced his tongue in random designs up and over the whole exposed region of my bare pussy—first this way, then that. He made delicious heart shapes in various sizes and smooth round circles that grew smaller and smaller, as if honing in on the bull's-eye of my clit until I was on the verge of swooning with pleasure. He pushed me up to the crest of climax again and again without letting me fall over the top until he was ready.

Raymond licked up and down once, quickly, as if to gauge how excited I was, and then he settled into a slower pace, using his tongue in meandering movements, electrifying every part of my sopping-wet sex. Each knowing flick of his tongue brought forth a flood of juices, and I imagined that Raymond's mouth was getting shiny wet, that his whole face might be coated with evidence of my pleasure when he was through. That vision turned me on so much that I groaned and raised my hips upward.

Immediately, he spoke into my pussy, telling me to calm down.

"So good," I told him. "It feels so fucking good."

His tongue flicked over my clit in a wordless answer that left me spinning. He gave me several quick licks in a row, and I grabbed his thick hair with both hands and pressed him even more firmly against my body. Raymond wriggled easily out of my grip, showing me once again that he was running this show. Resigned, I lay back down and let him work.

When we're apart, I make myself climax by mentally replaying the way Raymond pleases me with his lips and tongue. But this time was even better than previous encounters. That night, I found myself on the receiving end of the most amazing session of true oral worship I'd ever experienced. Around and around went Raymond's tongue before thrusting deep inside me to touch and stroke my most hidden and powerful points of pleasure.

"Oh, yes," I moaned, my hips starting to beat out a rhythm on the wooden table. "That feels delicious."

"This is only the appetizer," he insisted, inserting one finger deep into my slippery wet cunt. Then he flicked my clit with his thumb before going back to the job with his open, hungry mouth.

He wrapped his lips around my hard button and gave me long, wet kisses. I lost myself in the satisfying feeling of his strong hands caressing my ass, his warm skin against my body, his hot, wet breath playing over my clit like a sexual melody created just for me. I was getting blindingly close to orgasm, and the words were right on the tip of my tongue, when Raymond murmured, "I know you are. I know. Relax, Maria, just let it happen."

I felt weightless in his embrace as ribbons of ecstasy radiated out from the very center of my being. When he made me come the first time, I brought my legs around his neck, sealing my pussy against his face. There was no thought to my actions. I had to get as close as possible to his mouth. I slammed myself against him, holding on tight as he continued to trick his tongue up and down, devouring my clit and giving me every ounce of the pleasure I so desperately craved. My body worked without any commands from my brain as I tumbled into orgasm.

"Oh god," I sighed, my voice hoarse. "Oh, Ray. That's amazing."

I was certain he'd let me slide slowly back to reality after that, where I could catch my breath as I basked in the glow of my pleasure, but he didn't. Without saying a word, he continued, using a gentler touch. Paying particular care to the regions around my clit, he employed the flat of his tongue to make large, looping circles that reached all the way up to the ridge of my pubic bone, not approaching my pulsing clitoris at all. I floated in a sea of sexual sensations. My pussy was alive with mighty shudders that reverberated all the way to my fingertips, to the pulse point in the hollow of my throat. I started rocking my head back and forth, not telling him no, not believing that I could be experiencing this type of euphoria right after such a spectacular climax, as if my orgasm were being extended from seconds to minutes.

Then Raymond changed his tactics. He realized that I was

ready, and that I wanted it. I wanted to feel his mouth back where it belonged, pressed exactly to my demanding pearl. I came even louder the second time, and then I collapsed as if liquefied on the center of the table. But I realized, even in my haze of happiness, that something was definitely missing. I was the hungry one, so ravenously hungry that I couldn't wait another minute.

"I need your cock," I told Raymond, my voice husky with want. "I mean, I need it bad—"

Desperation must have been written on my face, because in an instant Raymond had stripped out of his clothes and pushed himself up on the table, with his knees close to my head. With a graceful gesture, he swiveled his hips so that his erection was poised perfectly over my parted lips.

I sighed with satisfaction. It was my turn to reciprocate, and I was more than ready to do so.

I slid my tongue along his shaft, and I felt his dick growing even larger. Raymond groaned urgently, but I wouldn't be rushed. I bestowed a long, slow, wet kiss upon the head of his cock before drawing in his rigid length. It felt wonderful to have my throat filled with his organ. I knew how turned on he was, and I understood exactly what he wanted me to do: to eat him from top to bottom, to devour every single inch.

It was my pleasure to do so. I swallowed around his girth, so that he could feel my throat's embrace, and then bobbed my head up and down, first slowly, then increasing the speed. I cradled his balls with one hand, and then used the other to work the spit-slicked shaft as I continued sucking.

I was dripping from having his hard cock in my mouth, even wetter than I'd gotten during my own two climaxes. I squirmed around impatiently as I swallowed him, and I thought about what it would feel like when he ultimately entered my cunt. He'd find an ocean of wetness and would swim in my juices with each plunge—but not yet. At that moment, it was all about Raymond's cock, which was consumed entirely by my hungry mouth.

After several minutes, I let Raymond work at his own rhythm, fucking my face, moving rapidly to catch up to me. I moved my hands to his hips and let him take what he wanted, which was my lips pursed around his shaft, his body pumping, moving ferociously as he felt the pleasure growing.

His cock seemed to swell with each forward thrust of his hips. I relaxed my throat as much as I could and used my tongue in a dragging motion along his shaft when he pulled out. Then, I used back-and-forth zigzags as his dick slipped back into my mouth.

"Oh, baby," he sighed, "your mouth is heavenly."

The compliment urged me onward, and he let me take control again, rocking up and down on his cock with a ferocious intensity rarely seen outside X-rated movies. It was my goal to make him feel completely conflicted—I wanted the pleasure of my actions to be so great that he didn't even want to come, that he'd want to remain in that ecstatic state of almost reaching orgasm for as long as he possibly could. When he sighed even deeper and said, "I can't hold off much longer," I really went to work, getting the entire length of his powerful prick all gleaming wet and slippery.

I understood how urgently he wanted to come, and I was ready to give him that great prize, letting him reach the dramatic heights he'd taken me to already. That was my plan—suck him right, suck him hard, make him feel so much pleasure he thinks he'll explode—

then make him actually explode. I wanted to drain every drop of his sweet juices and then get him hard and do it all over again.

I was so fixated on my work, and the intensity was so great, that I didn't immediately realize when Raymond moved and brought his mouth back to my pussy. Suddenly, I felt his hot breath on me, his tongue making those knowing circles on my tingling sex. I cried out, with my voice all muffled by his cock, and came in a sudden wave of vibrations on his tongue. At that same moment, he climaxed as well, filling my mouth with his milky semen.

I couldn't remember any sexual experience ever before being so intense. It was almost as if I lost consciousness for a second, but I came back around as I heard Raymond whispering, "So, do you think we should keep this item on the menu?"

My mouth was too full of his cock and come to respond verbally, but I nodded my agreement. This concept was definitely a winner: the indulgent decadence of all-you-can-eat nights—and all-you-can-be-eaten nights, too. I'd definitely be coming back for seconds.

Mouth Magic

MATTHEW EMERSON

Waking up to a blow job has got to be the sexiest thing I can imagine. Of course, until I met Susan, imagining was as far as I'd gotten. It wasn't like my other girlfriends had a problem with oral sex. Plenty of women enjoy sucking off their lovers, and some might even do it first thing in the morning, assuming they happen to be early risers. But not too many will actually plan a Sunday morning around it. That shows not just consideration for your man but a real passion for cock. Thankfully, Susan has that passion in spades. And starting with one fine weekend last year—a month after we'd met—that passion became a major part of our sex life.

The whole thing began as a delicious dream, an intense pleasure playing around the edges of my consciousness. When I finally opened my eyes, I still wasn't completely awake. I was on top of the sheets, bathed in warm summer sun and aware only of something warm gripping and releasing my cock, and a wet, subtle tickling on its head. I moaned with pleasure when I finally realized what was happening.

Susan was sprawled across my lower body, her fist around my prick, holding it steady while she licked and sucked. I had a massive case of morning wood, and Susan was encouraging it with her mouth. She circled the tip of my swollen head with her tongue, while slowly and rhythmically squeezing my shaft with her warm hand. Her long hair fell around my thighs, tickling my bare skin. All I could think to do was lie there, enjoying the delicious teasing.

Susan is twenty-five, four years younger than me. If you'd seen her right then, lying sprawled on the covers like a big sexy cat, you'd never have believed she's an accountant. Her body is long and lithe, tanned to a beautiful light brown that goes wonderfully with her platinum-blonde hair. She's got long legs and an incredible ass. Her boobs are perfect little handfuls, tipped with large coral-colored nipples that were as erect as my dick.

"God, that feels good," I breathed, anxious to keep her going. But Susan was obviously in no hurry to stop or even make me come. She simply smiled and kept on licking, like my cock was a big lollipop. Every time her tongue made contact with my skin, I got a delicious little shock, a tiny jolt that brought me further and further out of sleep and deeper into exquisite horniness. Hypnotized, I lay there twitching, reveling in those incredible sensations.

Susan's own arousal finally got the better of her. She hung her head over my dick for a long while, warming it with her breath and clenching and unclenching her fist around it. It was like she was considering what to do next. Finally, she whispered, "Do you want to fuck my mouth?"

"Yeah," I said. I could barely speak. I was no longer afraid of coming before I was ready; I felt like I had reached a state that somehow transcended my body's usual responses. But I certainly did want to fuck Susan's mouth; right then I wanted that more than anything in the world.

"Say it. I want to hear you say it."

She was in total control of me at that moment. I was ready to do anything she said, whenever she said to do it.

"Yeah, I want to fuck your mouth. I want to fuck it."

Susan made a kind of delirious growling noise and then went down on me. She put her mouth over my cock and closed her pink lips around its root. For a single perfect moment, my meat was pulsing in the damp heat of my girl's mouth. She sucked, drawing greedily on my cock like it was a cigar. I felt the inner walls of her cheeks and palate close in on me, as well as the soft, slight roughness of her tongue.

There was nothing teasing about this sensation; this was the same satisfying feeling I got when I buried my prick in Susan's wet pussy. This was fucking, and my body responded to it as such. Gasping, I reached up for the headboard and held on for dear life. My hips jerked for a moment, then settled into a series of rolling thrusts. My body prickled with sweat, but the fever of my arousal was cooled by the occasional delicious breeze from our window.

I watched Susan's head bob as she sucked me. Up and down it went, her blonde hair shining in the sunlight. She went at my cock like this was the last chance she'd ever have to blow one. Every couple of seconds she would let me loose, just long enough to snatch a ragged breath. Then she'd give me a fierce, hungry look and go back to work.

Soon I felt the signs that I was approaching orgasm—a trembling itch in my balls and a delicious ache in the base of my spine. I began thrusting wildly into Susan's mouth, bracing my feet on the mounded sheets. She moaned a little, tiny puffs of air escaping between the sides of her mouth and my meat, before she eased up on the intensity of her sucking. She slowly raised her head so that, just as slowly, my shaft slid through her moist lips. My cockhead lingered deliciously between them for a moment. She gave it a tiny lick with her tongue and then set it free. A second later she began the whole process over again, seizing my dick in her mouth and pulling it upward while I gasped and swore.

It was agonizing and delicious, a teasing, excruciating torture designed both to coax my orgasm from me and hold it off until the last possible second. I loved it, even as it was driving me out of my fucking mind.

Eventually, things came—no pun intended—to a head. I felt precome seeping out of me. I knew I could no longer hold back my orgasm, and Susan must have realized it as well. She gave me one last, loving look, and then she brought me home: she took my shaft all the way in her mouth again, sucking and slurping while she used her hands to cup my balls and lightly massage them.

I don't know what finally did it; the sensations were exquisite, like music being played on my body. But the sight of Susan's beautiful face—her eyes shut and her long lashes trembling—triggered a deep response. I cried out and my cream fountained up. When Susan released me, she had a droplet of semen on her lips. She smiled lovingly and swallowed my load.

"More," she crooned, and I somehow obliged. Susan squeezed

my cock and caught a second, even larger spurt in her open hand.

By then I felt not just empty, but hollowed out. I finally allowed myself to let go of the headboard and fell onto the damp sheets, breathing as hard as if I'd run a marathon. I was vaguely aware of Susan leaving the room and the sound of water running in our bathroom. I must have dozed a little, because the next thing I knew, Susan was back on the bed, cleaning my cock with a wet washcloth.

"Wow," I murmured.

"Pretty amazing," Susan agreed, setting the cloth aside and climbing up to put her arms around me. "You're so responsive," she breathed, whispering the words in my ear. "So sensual. I wanted to do something like this with you from the very first night we made love."

"Why didn't you?" I asked.

"I had to wait for the right moment. And besides," she said with a smile, "it's better when it's a surprise. Isn't it?"

I had to agree that it was.

In the days that followed, Susan and I talked a lot about our experience, and about her love of sucking cock. Her upbringing had been rather conservative, and she had emerged into adulthood with the idea that certain sexual acts were strictly forbidden. Of course, this had created in her an unquenchable fascination with those acts, and a deep desire to try them out for herself.

As a result, she had been a wild child during her college years. She hadn't exactly been promiscuous, she explained, but when she managed to hook up with guys, she took every opportunity to experiment. She had played with bondage and S/M, enjoyed a few threesomes and had several flings with other girls. But throughout it all, she discovered that oral sex was her truest passion.

"I just love cock," she told me the next evening, giggling over a glass of chilled white wine. "I love cock the way some men love pussy. I can't leave it alone. And sucking you yesterday was absolute heaven. I knew I didn't have to hurry and that you enjoyed what I was doing to you as much as I enjoyed doing it. And when you came…mmm. It was the sexiest thing I've ever seen!"

Susan licked the rim of her glass, staring at me with her beautiful blue eyes. I started squirming in my chair, my cock slowly growing rigid. "I'm so glad we found each other," she purred. "You're my favorite indulgence."

"I don't suppose you'd care to indulge yourself a little right now?" I said as I smiled.

Susan laughed. "Well, there *is* something I've always wanted to try. A little technique I understand is quite devastating."

Barely able to keep from panting, I asked her what she had in mind. She dropped me a slow wink, and then without another word, she got up and padded into the kitchen. I heard her rattling dishes, opening the refrigerator and running the microwave. I squirmed a little more, wondering what on earth she was up to. I was patient, though, knowing it would be something worth waiting for.

When Susan reemerged, she was carrying her wineglass, topped off with more chardonnay, the sides fogged with condensation. In her other hand was a steaming mug of tea.

"Thirsty?" I asked, raising an eyebrow.

"Uh-huh," she nodded, grinning. "Thirsty for you." She curled up at my feet, set the drinks on either side of us, and put her hands on my knees. "Get ready," she whispered, pushing them apart so that my erection was visible through my trousers.

Susan leaned forward and kissed my hard-on through the thin material of my pants. I groaned a little, hips rising up slightly in my seat. My cock felt as heavy and stiff as a lead pipe, threatening to rip free of its prison and bury itself in Susan's mouth. I reached for my fly to help the process along, but Susan touched my hand lightly, shaking her head with a sly smile.

"Just relax," she whispered, firmly placing my wrists on the chair's armrests. "Let me take care of you, baby."

Before I could say a word, she went back to kissing my crotch. Something about the way she did it was making me crazy. Her slow, languorous pace made me anticipate her every move. She gently mouthed my erection through my pants, and my cock was so hard it ached.

Finally, after what felt like hours of this pleasurable torment, Susan bit my fly and gradually worked the zipper down with her teeth. Then she used her hand to maneuver my cock out into the air. When she kissed the naked flesh, I thought I was going to shoot immediately, but my luck—and my load—managed to hold. I groaned as once again my prick disappeared into Susan's mouth, and I settled back in my chair for a ride into heaven.

This time, though, Susan cut the ride short—if only temporarily. I must have given her a truly anguished look, because she laughed out loud.

"Can't a girl take a second to wet her whistle?" She giggled, reaching for her glass. "You know, all this work makes me thirsty." With that, she took a sizable mouthful of wine. Then, before I could ready myself, she caught my dick in her luscious, chilled mouth. The sensation was unbelievable. I'd never felt anything like it. It wasn't painful or unpleasant at all, but the unexpected shock of it made me cry out. My balls tightened up in response to the deliciousness.

"Aww, was that too cold? Don't want you to catch a chill." Susan lifted her mug of tea, blew on it and sipped. This time I knew what was coming, but I still wasn't quite prepared. After the cold, the heated confines of her mouth were indescribable. It woke up my nerves and had me thrusting my hips so hard that Susan had to set the mug down to avoid spilling the tea.

I made it through three more demonstrations of Susan's hot/cold trick. The third time I got "hot," I lost it completely, my load flooding her warm mouth with so much cream that she had to pull her head away and swallow. Then she took me between her lips again, sucking until my balls were totally drained.

"Delicious," she said, and then she smiled and chased my load with another swallow of cold wine.

The following weeks were incredibly hot ones as Susan tried out one incredible oral delight after another on my willing cock. Naturally, I wanted to reciprocate—and not only because I loved this woman and what she did to me. I wanted to experience this amazing pleasure from the other side. I had eaten pussy before, of course, but now I was positively hungry for it. I longed to taste Susan's juices and drive her crazy with my tongue.

But Susan was surprisingly demure when I proposed eating her pussy. She kept putting me off.

"I'm so sensitive down there," she said. "I love it, but I'm afraid I'd make too much noise."

"Like the way you make me scream?" I grinned. It took quite a bit of teasing, but finally I got her to agree. And by then I had a few ideas of how I could make our evening truly a night to remember.

It was a beautiful summer night, and we prepared for our special evening with dinner at a local four-star restaurant. Afterward, we enjoyed some drinks and dancing. Then, at last, we went home—and to bed.

Susan's pussy was snug and sweet smelling. I spent a long time licking it, teasing her plump clit out of hiding. She wasn't kidding when she said she was sensitive; she made the most amazing noises as I tongued her, lying back and biting one finger to stifle her moans as little tremors ran all down the length of her body.

Using my lips and teeth, I sucked and pulled gently at her lower lips. I was trying to establish a sensual rhythm, the same way she had made me jerk and thrust, and soon enough she was dancing to my tune, her long limbs making soft sighing noises as they rubbed against the smooth sheets. She bent her knees and spread them as wide as they would go. She clapped a hand around the back of my head, urging me in a throaty voice to eat her harder, to nibble at her thighs, to lick her clit, to make her scream with delight.

Eventually, she did scream. I felt her straining toward climax, rocking her ass on the bed as though trying to build up momentum. When her orgasm finally came, the force of it shook her to her very core, making her swear and shudder and bite her lip.

That was the moment I had been waiting for. I kissed her pussy softly, knowing I needed to be careful because she would be even more sensitive now. When I knew she was ready for another round—and it didn't take long—I turned quickly around, straddling her body in a classic sixty-nine so that my hard cock dangled temptingly before her lips.

Susan seized it immediately, closing her mouth on my dick and sucking blissfully. The intensity of it was fantastic; it made me all the more ravenous for her. I went back to work on her pussy, gently separating her legs once again and pulling at her lips with my own. If Susan had been responsive before, now she was doubly so. Something about having my cock in her mouth while being eaten seemed to send her into an absolute sexual frenzy. She snuffled and growled around my dick, reaching up to caress my balls as I licked and sucked her sweet fruit.

"Gimme it," she mumbled, her voice barely audible as she lapped at me. "Gimme your load."

"I'll give it to you, all right," I whispered. I was working her pussy with the greatest possible delicacy. I wanted to tickle her, to make her crazy until I knew that she was ready for what I had in mind.

I waited until she released my cock in order to get a breath. I broke our position and turned around so that I now faced her. Susan pouted adorably for a brief moment, disappointed that her lollipop had been taken from her. But her disappointment was short-lived; as I plunged my cock—slick with Susan's saliva—into her pussy, her eyes widened and she made a low, crying noise that gradually turned into a growl, then became something between a roar and delighted, uncontrollable laughter.

God, it was good! It was the best fucking I think either of us had ever experienced up to that point. I moved slowly, pumping in and out of her while she met every thrust of my hips with the smooth motion of her own. With my patient movements, she came for a second time, quivering and wailing as the muscles in her fluttering pussy clamped around my dick. By then, of course, I couldn't have staved off my own orgasm any longer if I'd wanted to. I surrendered to the delicious feeling of my load emptying into Susan's pussy.

When we finished, I slid off her and we moved into each other's arms, exhausted and deliriously happy. We lay together quietly for a while, but eventually we started talking. Susan, unsurprisingly, was already making plans for another oral workout—and I couldn't think of a better way to spend the weekend.

Local Delicacies

Evan Wilcox

"So, you're interested in eating locally?" the brunette woman purred as I took a seat next to her in the crowded auditorium. There was only one space left in the tiny but packed community center, and it was right by her side.

"Definitely," I responded automatically as I slipped off my denim jacket. It took me a moment to get settled, then I relaxed in the metal folding chair. I'd had an hour-long drive, and my mind was still on traffic. But when I turned my head and fully caught her appearance, I did a double take. She was beautiful, with sleek dark hair pinned up in a neat twist, deep-green eyes and a feisty expression. Now I nodded fiercely. "Very, *very* interested."

It was true. I've always been intrigued by food—from organic, to gourmet, to foreign cuisine. This is why I had originally decided to drive from the city to this small seaside community to attend a meeting focused on eating locally. The idea behind the concept is to only consume food grown within a hundred-mile radius from your own front door. The flyer for the event stated: *Eat locally. It's seven o'clock. Do you know where your food comes from? Stop by the community center on Friday night and find out. Together, we can change the world, one bite at a time.*

Of course, this ideal is fairly easy to observe in the farm-rich environment where the workshop was being held, while it is decidedly more difficult to do in an urban location. However, regardless of my interest in what the experts had to say, or my personal faithful commitment to maintaining a healthy lifestyle, my brain had switched from food to sex as soon as I viewed my new neighbor.

The stunning woman stood out amidst the country girls in their faded denim and the hippie chicks dressed in head-to-toe tie-dye. This minx was wearing a short, red velvet dress, black-patterned stockings and patent-leather boots. As soon as our eyes met, I felt my cock harden.

"I think it's a great idea," she said softly to me as we waited for the talk to begin. She indicated the charts posted up on the wall behind the podium, depicting how eating locally is good for health, the environment and the community's economic growth. I found myself grateful for all of the other people who had chosen to come out on this early autumn night—forcing the chairs so close together that I could feel her breath against my cheek as she spoke and smell the subtle scent of her perfume, which was as light and sweet as honeysuckle. "It just makes sense," she continued.

"Yes," I told her, realizing that I'd probably agree to anything as I focused on her rich, ruby-red lips, pink cheeks and those warm green eyes. "Definitely." There were platters of colorful sliced fruits and vegetables being passed around, but even as I tore myself away from her gaze in order to admire the array of fresh produce laid out in a decorative fan display, I was already picturing my tongue sampling the lady at my side.

Simply put, the girl just seemed to exude sex.

When she crossed her legs, I caught a glimpse of bare skin underneath the hem of her dress. If I were a cartoon character, my eyes would have bugged out of my skull. She was wearing thigh-high stockings that emphasized the length of her long, lean legs, and when she moved, I caught sight of the band of black lace at the top of one stocking. I had to swallow hard and look away once more, willing myself to concentrate on the subject matter at hand.

Food, I thought. *Not fucking. Food.*

The keynote speaker took his position in front of the group, and immediately began talking in a monotonous manner, explaining in great detail about the yin and yang of organic produce, but all of those words became so much background static—white noise.

When the pretty brunette shifted again, I couldn't help but notice how milky white her skin was, and how firm and silky her thighs looked from my view. She was undeniably hard to resist.

I ran my hand through my hair, pushing it out of my eyes, and did my best to concentrate on what was being said. I'd come to learn, not to get laid. That's what I told myself, anyway. But my brain—and my cock, which kept throbbing unhelpfully in my jeans—had other ideas entirely.

"Food grown locally is by definition fresher," the speaker intoned, "and far more luscious."

Immediately, my thoughts returned to the desirable woman at my side. *Yes,* I thought. *Luscious.*

"Eating locally is one way for concerned environmentalists to make a stand. And it's not difficult at all, especially with food this delectable."

Mmm, I thought now. *Delectable.*

The girl at my side shifted once more, and her thigh touched mine. A flare of electric energy burst through me. Had she meant to touch me? I hoped so.

"Eating locally is something that people can start doing immediately."

That's right, I thought. *Immediately.* I had become desperate to start eating locally that very second, and to begin between the infinitely desirable legs of the vixen on my right. I had a vision of going down on my knees on the well-worn wooden floor, pushing her scarlet dress to her waist and pressing my face to her sex. But even in an open-minded environment that was pushing local eating, I thought perhaps this would be taking things a little too far.

Just then, her thigh brushed mine once more, and I wondered if she sensed how aroused she was making me with each little squirm in her chair. Was she simply trying to get comfortable on the hard metal chair, or was she truly a naughty little imp intent on teasing me?

"With a trained eye, you can tell local food from that which has been grown elsewhere and trucked in," the speaker droned on. "Local food has a glow to it, a ripeness..."

A glow, echoed in my head. *A ripeness.* When the brunette put her hand on my leg, she answered my unasked question. Clearly, she wasn't only shifting around for comfort. I thought that perhaps she was as horny—I mean hungry—as I was. Her soft hand rested gently on my thigh, and then she squeezed me once, as if testing the ripeness of fruit, just as the speaker was suggesting. I closed my eyes, stifling a groan that wanted desperately to escape from my throat. I had a feeling that heads would swivel in my direction if I moaned as wolfishly as I desired.

How had we sped to this point so quickly? I have no idea. Perhaps the charts had gotten to her. The speaker had moved on to talking about paying attention to the types of delicious treats to be discovered in your very own neighborhood. Did this girl think that meant men, as well? I wasn't going to question my luck.

When the group broke for a twenty-minute intermission, the sultry brunette beckoned me to follow her outside.

"If you'd like," she said softly. "I can give you a tour of the greenhouse. I mean, that's if you're really interested in eating locally, which I hope you are."

I nodded. In truth, I would have followed her anywhere.

Behind the community center was a small, neatly arranged organic garden. The lady headed down a pebbled path that led directly to a greenhouse way off in the rear, and I followed quickly, so excited I could hardly breathe.

When I opened the door to the greenhouse, she had already hoisted herself up on one of the shelves, her red dress a cloud of velvet hiked up to her slim waist, her long racehorse legs spread in the exact pose I had envisioned during the speech. But this was real, not a fantasy. She had on a pair of cotton-candy-pink panties edged in delicate white lace. I sucked in my breath at the sight of her. She was so damn luscious, as edible as any of the plants surrounding her. And far more delicious, if I guessed correctly.

The look in her eyes let me know that she wanted me, wanted me as desperately, as urgently, as ravenously as I wanted her. She gazed at me with a becoming petal-like blush coloring her cheeks, then nodded down to herself, and I hurried the few steps separating us to stand between her spread legs. It was time to dine!

There were no words needed. I knelt before her and pressed my face to her panty-clad pussy, drinking in the scent of her. With one lick, I was able to actually taste her through the thin fabric of her panties. As I nibbled on the lady's plump pussy lips—I heard the speaker's words echo once more in my head: *ripe, juicy, delectable.* I savored every moment, tasting the sweet flow of her juices through her panties, and I had to agree with the speaker's concept: eating locally was definitely good for this particular man's taste buds. She was sweet, and the abundance of juices dampening her panties let me know that I was definitely pleasing her, even though I'd thought only of my own appetite.

She needn't have made a sound to let me know that she approved of my actions, but to my great satisfaction, my new partner was anything but silent. She leaned back against the glass wall of the greenhouse and moaned, lifting her hips and letting me know that she was ready for me to slip her undies down her thighs, over her shiny boots and off. I did so immediately, intently focused on the dessert spread out before me. The fact that her stockings were still in place turned me on even more.

I used my fingers to part her shaved pussy lips, and then, even though I was focused on the finish line, I made myself take a second to admire her: the glistening wetness of her sex; the pretty rose-hued folds of her pussy. She was like a hothouse flower, so warm and damp—so willing to open.

"Please," she whimpered, shivering all over with excitement. "Please!"

This was something the speaker hadn't mentioned. I mean, how often does your dinner beg you to dine on it? I smiled at my own silent joke before taking pity on her. Knowing precisely what she needed, I dipped my tongue inside her and then swirled it around her clit. The sensation of my wet tongue on her bare skin drove her instantly wild. She groaned deeply and arched her back. I felt her muscles grow taut as she tensed in desperate anticipation of her climax. When I'd tasted her through her panties, she had grown extremely aroused, but that was nothing compared to how hot and wet she was at that moment.

She gripped my shoulders forcefully, her hands clawing at me through my jacket as she pressed herself more aggressively against my open mouth.

"Oh god that feels good," she murmured.

"Yeah?" I whispered. "You like that?" I wanted to hear her talk, and she seemed to understand my desire.

"So good," she continued. "The way your tongue feels against me." I made a hungry noise, urging her to continue. "And the way your mouth moves—" Her words trailed off into a sigh.

"You're so sweet," I responded, unable to keep silent. "So damn sweet."

"Please don't stop," she begged, made crazy by the momentary lapse of my tongue against her when I'd moved aside to talk to her.

No, I wouldn't stop again. Not until I'd savored every drop of her delicious juices. I continued to trail my tongue in languid spirals around her throbbing clit, and then interspersed those circles with little hungry nips at her inner thighs and swollen pussy lips. She cooed as I began to eat her ever more vigorously, and I understood she was ready for an even firmer touch. I pressed my face hard against her, drinking from her, and in seconds, she moaned louder than she had yet, and then shuddered hard. I knew from the quivering flesh pressed against my mouth that she was coming.

I wished I could have seen her face when she came, but I was unwilling to let go of her clit. It was locked between my lips and trapped right where I wanted it. I sucked on her hard, and she wrapped her thighs all the way around my head, holding me to her as her orgasm broke over her. Again and again, she bucked toward me, until finally those sublime contractions subsided and she let me loose.

I sat back on the dirt floor, feeling infinitely pleased with myself. I had made her come in such a short amount of time, but I felt as if I'd just dined on the most exquisite five-course meal. My face was coated with the glossy juices from her pussy; my chin and lips slick with the musky evidence of her arousal.

When I looked up at her, I saw a glow of satisfaction on her face and felt even more proud that I'd been the one to make her feel that way. And then I leaned back on my hands and waited. I didn't know what she'd do next, what she might be ready for. I was sure the speech had begun again in the community center. For one pathetic moment, I thought she'd simply drop her dress and head back to the workshop, but to my great relief, she didn't. After catching her breath, she pushed herself off the shelf and indicated that I take her place. I raised my eyebrows at her, and she gave me a sexy half smirk, then bent and kissed my lips. She took a step back from me, then licked her own lips, tasting herself and clearly relishing that delightful flavor.

"Your turn." She grinned, and my heart beat so loud I was sure that she could hear it. *My turn.* I had only the barest fantasy of what that might mean. "Don't make me wait," she demanded. "I'm hungry." Her eyes roamed over my body, lingering on the obvious bulge in my slacks, and I couldn't have waited another second if I'd tried. I stood up and pulled hard on my button fly, and as soon as I had popped opened my jeans, she was on me, slipping one hand into my pants, gripping the root of my cock between her warm fingers. Her hand felt amazing on my naked skin, and she worked me as if she knew exactly what I craved. As I stared at her in awe, she jacked my cock once, twice, three times, as if testing the girth and the heft of it, and then she gave me another one of those ravenous smiles and knelt before me.

"Oh god," I moaned as she began to suck me. I felt my own knees start to buckle as pleasure flooded through me, and I was grateful for the support of the shelf behind my back. Her lips—the first things I'd noticed about her—were highly glossed in red. That lipstick smeared as soon as she got the first inch of my cock into her mouth. I loved the way the color looked on her and loved the way the glossy lipstick smeared on my shaft even more. She hadn't lied. She was definitely hungry—hungry for me, anyway. She treated me with finesse, her delicate hand cradling my sensitive balls, and her mouth bobbing up and down on my rod, trying to bring her mouth down to the very base, to swallow my shaft whole.

"Oh," I moaned. "Oh, please," not even sure what I was asking for, but unable to keep quiet. She worked me like a powerful sucking engine, but even better than the way she drank from my cock was the way her eyes kept locking onto mine. I gazed down at her, my hands twining in her hair, pulling the strands loose from the once-neat up-do, and she met my stare, green eyes looking up at me, locking on my expression of lust and unwilling to look away.

I rocked my hips forward, taking over from her, guiding my cock between her parted lips. And suddenly, it was too much for me. I couldn't take any more. Not of this game, anyway. I wanted something a little different—something even more fulfilling.

Pulling back from her, I said, "Lie down on the ground."

She didn't hesitate to obey my command. Some girls would have. The fancy city girls I see every day on the hills of San Francisco would not have even considered lying down on the dirt floor. They would have refused to get their clothes messy, but not this girl. Even though she didn't look like the nutty-crunchy type, not in her velvet and thigh-highs and those stunning boots, she had no problem sprawling out on the floor of the greenhouse.

Moonlight filtered in from above, and I maneuvered my body so that I was poised over her mouth, slipping my cock once again between her lips, but now I was able to press my face into her pussy, to taste her honey once more.

That was divine—feeling her warm mouth suckle me in the same rhythm, the same fucking beat with which my tongue was teasing her clit. I flicked my tongue against her, and she swallowed hard. I brought my lips tight around her throbbing button, and she mimicked my motion, tricking her tongue in tantalizing circles right around the head of my pulsing cock. At first, she acted as if my cock were a lollipop or an ice-cream cone, licking me slowly and lusciously. But when I thrust my tongue inside her pussy, she began to fiercely deep-throat me.

"Oh god," I moaned, pulling away for a moment to catch my breath. Yet I couldn't stay away for long. No man would have been able to. She was too succulent, too juicy. I needed to have her taste on my tongue, needed to lap up any drops I'd missed.

I pressed my face against her soft thighs and searched every inch of her soft skin for that unreal ambrosia.

Soon we were moving in tandem, working together, sucking and drinking, until I moaned once more; my face was pressed so hard to the split between her legs that my growl of lust was lost against her body. "I'm going to—" I groaned. "I am almost there—"

"Don't wait," she hissed. "Let yourself go."

And I did. I was unstoppable. I fucked her mouth hard, before shooting down her throat and understanding in some distant realm of my brain that she was coming with me. I could hardly believe that I'd managed to take her over the edge yet again.

She swallowed every last drop that I had in me, and then gave me one more long, hard lick from root to tip. A final shudder wracked my body, and I moaned once more, then rolled off her onto my back, staring up through the glass ceiling at the full autumn moon above us. The sweet brunette twisted around so that we both faced in the same direction, and I put one arm around her and held her tightly against my chest.

We were down there on the dirt floor, surrounded by the scent of peat moss and lush vegetation—cradled in the still night air and the twinkle of the stars. We could have been in Eden—instead of in a small community greenhouse. Regardless of our actual location, I felt that we were truly in paradise.

There was no longer a question of whether or not we were going to return to the speech; not with bits of hay in our hair and dirt on our knees. Instead, I squired her out to the parking lot and then my car. She smiled as she reached to snag a flyer that someone had placed on my windshield.

I looked at the pink paper before she folded it up and tucked it into the glove compartment, and I had to chuckle. It read: *Eating locally—It's definitely an idea whose time has come.*

Tongue Travels

ANDY KESSLER

Five hours is an extremely long time to be stuck waiting in an airport, even in these days of slow-moving lines and heightened security. In an effort to save as much time as possible, I hadn't checked a bag and had my e-ticket at the ready, but being grounded by inclement weather was an unexpected wrinkle. Still, by the time I and the other would-be passengers were informed that the remainder of that night's flights had been canceled, I don't think anyone was surprised. A flat-screen TV at the departure gate had been playing weather reports pretty much nonstop, and the words "worst snowstorm of the year" had already been used more than once. However, that didn't stop some people from getting irritated and blaming the desk attendants as though they'd had foreknowledge of what the tower eventually decided.

I, on the other hand, was feeling nothing but blissful satisfaction. What had been a set of unfortunate circumstances for most of my fellow travelers, had turned into a felicitous occasion for me. This is how it happened: as we sat in our rows of interlocking chairs, we stayed glued to the local news while we waited for some sort of pronouncement, all of us growing more anxious by the moment. Just as I was beginning to wonder if I'd make it to Pittsburgh in time to prepare for my morning presentation, the woman sitting to my right asked if I'd watch her stuff so that she could go buy herself some gum and a magazine.

Saying yes was a no-brainer because I'd already been watching her "stuff" for a while. Checking out the sexy brunette had been a good distraction, but I would have noticed her regardless of the situation. Even though she was wearing bulky winter clothes, I could see that she kept herself in great shape; her cable-knit sweater did little to hide a pair of large, firm breasts. Below that, her waist was slender, but when she stood up I could see that her ass was generously plump.

All I could do as I sat there was imagine sinking my fingers into the plush flesh of her bottom cheeks as she pressed those tits against me. I guess I should also mention that she had an extremely pretty face, with long-lashed hazel eyes and pink-hued lips that displayed two rows of perfectly straight pearly whites whenever she smiled, which she was doing as she waited for my answer. To be honest, it was her mouth that I was most interested in, because her request had interrupted a fantasy in which it was wrapped around my dick.

Caught off guard, I shifted and cleared my throat, hoping that she hadn't noticed the bulge in the front of my pants; I had stirred myself into such a state that I thought my cock might literally burst.

I quickly nodded my assent and she hurried off, leaving me to my fantasies of fellatio, at least until she returned and reclaimed her seat. After thanking me and telling me her name—Erin—she offered me a stick of her gum, which I took. For a while after, we made the usual chitchat of strangers when they first meet, but when it became obvious that we wouldn't be going anywhere anytime soon, we headed to the airport bar.

It was there, over cocktails, that we began to loosen up, and as the conversation got more personal, we started touching each other casually, until my hand was on her upper arm and she was absentmindedly stroking my thigh through my jeans. It had grown warm in the semi-crowded room, so she had taken off her bulky sweater, giving me a good peek at the large tits straining at her camisole. I could also see the outlines of her nipples, which practically poked holes through the black spandex top, and I hoped that meant she was turned on and not just chilly, because god knows how aroused I'd gotten!

It definitely seemed like she was flirting with me. As we talked, she kept licking her lips enticingly, until they were entirely clean of gloss and yet still unbearably sexy. I barely heard a word of what she was saying because all I could do was picture them—and the pink tongue of which she kept giving me glimpses—doing all sorts of wicked things to my dick. My own mouth watered incessantly as I went on to picture myself returning the favor, using my own tongue on her succulent cunt, and for about the hundredth time since I'd met Erin, I wished we were anywhere other than in an airport.

As I struggled to keep up my end of the conversation, all I could think about was burying my head between her thighs and licking her pussy until she screamed. That's why, when she excused herself to go to the ladies' room with what I was certain looked like a wink, it only took a moment of lust-fueled consideration before I hastily grabbed our carry-ons and followed her in hot pursuit. When I got to the restroom, I waited for a moment outside the door, and then, when the coast was clear, I ducked into that place where few guys had been and hoped I hadn't seriously misread her signals.

My footsteps echoed in the otherwise empty room, until the door to the large stall at the very end opened and Erin's head popped out. "I thought you'd never get here." She giggled as she motioned me inside, throwing her arms around my neck as soon as we were locked in. Pressing her lips to mine, she slipped her tongue into my open mouth, so I reached around to knead her asscheeks while she mashed her glorious tits against my chest. I was grinding my erection against her, so she reached down, gave it a squeeze and then began working open my jeans with nimble fingers. As she pulled out my turgid dick and began a lazy rhythm of pumping it in her tightened fist, I scrambled to get into her pants, too. Finally, with her open waistband barely past her hips, I slid my hand into her panties to slip my finger between her labia and stroke her sleek inner lips.

Erin's petals peeled back at my touch, and for a moment, she leaned against my hand as her breathing got slower and heavier. A minute later, she abruptly pulled herself off my fingers, so I brought them to my mouth to suck off her tangy juices as I waited to see what she'd do next. Mesmerized, I watched as she lowered the toilet lid and climbed onto it, bringing herself eye level with my erect cock. She held my shaft tightly at the root and contemplated it for a moment, and we both watched as a drop of precome oozed from the tiny slit in the tip.

That, apparently, was all the invitation she needed to dig in. My body tensed as she stuck out her sexy pink tongue and dragged it over my knob, swiping up the milky drop in the process. With a dramatic lick of her lips, she put on a show of *oohing* and *aahing* over the delicious treat of my dick, and in response, I surged forward uncontrollably, bumping her mouth with my cockhead. She immediately opened wide to envelop my mushroom-shaped tip, and after giving it a good, long suck, she swabbed her tongue around its circumference until my hips bucked back and forth.

I have to admit that I totally lost it. As she licked and sucked on the end of my prick, I writhed so much that I had no choice but to grab onto her head for support. Without really meaning to, I began force-feeding her my prodigious length, the ridge beneath my crown gliding along her tongue as she relaxed her throat muscles to allow my entry. Looking down at the top of her head, I contemplated my incredible luck: a half hour earlier, I'd been minding my own business while waiting to board a plane, and now I was in the ladies' room having my cock sucked with the kind of skill and enthusiasm I'd only before seen in porn flicks. Erin was definitely zealous, soon releasing a series of loud moans that had her throat vibrating against my sensitive flesh, which, in turn, raised the level of my arousal yet another notch. She was looking up at me, begging for more with her eyes because her voice had been silenced by my dick, so I obliged her by continuing to press forward, feeding her another inch.

In seconds, her nose was buried in my pubic hair and her chin rested against my testicles. Then, almost as quickly, her mouth was gone, leaving my dick bobbing in the open air of the restroom stall. Groaning throatily, I dug my fingers into her scalp as I guided her back onto my shaft, and she swallowed me even more easily this time. After that, she began demonstrating all of the miracles she could perform with her talented mouth, and my asscheeks began flexing with the undulations of my hips.

Maintaining a firm grip on Erin's head, I directed her movements as I closed my eyes and concentrated on the actions of her tongue. It was difficult, but while she sucked me, I was attempting to keep an ear out for announcements regarding our flight. Though now I was hoping it would be delayed further, maybe even canceled, because all I had to look forward to at its end was an early morning business meeting, whereas here in the bathroom, I could foresee an orgasm and, hopefully, the sweet taste of pussy.

The PA system remained silent for the duration, and in an even bigger stroke of luck, only one person entered the restroom, and she left a few moments later. Regardless, we both froze at the sound of the door opening, waiting with bated breath until we heard the sound of water splashing in the sink. My shaft never ceased pulsing against the flat of Erin's tongue the entire time. Opening my eyes, I glanced down to see her cheeks bulging around my dick, which seriously tested my patience, so as soon as we heard the door click shut, I picked up right where I'd left off, pumping into the tight ring she formed with her lips.

She remained as still as a statue so I could fuck her face, and I increased the pace of my thrusts into her mouth. I was trying to hurry up and finish, in case we had to rush out for our flight, and because I was also concerned that I might not have the time to return my partner's oral favors. Then I realized I might not have to: as my balls drew up against my pelvis in preparation to overflow, I once again felt her throat vibrating around my throbbing shaft. When I glanced down, I saw that she had one hand working busily between her thighs, pleasuring her own pussy even as she persisted in deep-throating me.

Oh, my fucking god, I thought to myself as I took in that incredible sight, and then I realized that I was still racing against the clock and should probably get a move on. So, as Erin's fingers moved in and out of her cunt, I dug my own fingers into her scalp to hold her head still as I shoved into her mouth one last time. A generous helping of hot, white cream spewed forth from my dick, and that crafty little cocksucker didn't miss a beat with either her hands or her tightly pursed lips. No, she kept on gulping, her throat repeatedly constricting as I coated it with my seed, and then she even milked me for a few drops that I hadn't known I had left to give. All the while, her delicate hand moved in her lap, her fingers thrusting in and out of her slippery hole and also brushing against her clit, until finally she gave a quake and moaned loudly around my shaft, which kept me hard for a few minutes longer.

As my cock started softening, the loudspeaker finally crackled to life. A representative of the airline announced that all further flights that evening—including ours—had been canceled, so we hustled to rearrange ourselves as the voice went on to say that some of the motels in the area still had vacancies, and that priority would be given to those who were willing to share. Erin and I looked at each other, and without speaking a decision was made. She was still licking my come from her lips as we rushed out to the gate, and my dick was already once again at half-mast in anticipation of our spending the rest of the night together, and in accommodations more private—and comfortable—than an airport rest room.

She already had her cell phone out and was nodding as she listened to someone on the other end. "I got us a room," she mouthed and just the sight of those lips—probably still a little tacky with my semen—as they moved soundlessly sent my brain into overdrive. Blood from the far reaches of my body coursed rapidly through my veins, and all of that pressure seemed to converge at my cock, which was soon once again ramrod stiff. My erection throbbed against my thigh as we hurried our way through the airport to a waiting hotel shuttle that seemed to take forever to get to our destination, although the ride was only twenty minutes long.

Also, it didn't help that Erin stroked the outline of my shaft through my jeans the entire time and kept licking her luscious lips and murmuring to me about how they still tasted like my salty load. My pulse raced wildly as I prayed for a quick end to our trip, and the pounding in my ears matched the rhythm of the bus's windshield wipers doing battle against the still-falling snow. Finally, when I was certain I would explode, we reached the hotel. Erin checked us in as quickly as she could, heartlessly ignoring the plaintive looks of other stranded travelers camped out in the motel lobby.

It was obvious that she was as worked up as I was, and with key in hand, we rushed to our room and immediately started tearing off each other's clothes. However, I was unable to wait until she was entirely nude. As soon as her sweater and cami were shed, I lowered my head to her magnificent breasts. Her rosy nipples stiffened as I swirled my tongue around them and nibbled gently. She began writhing against my face as she shimmied out of her jeans and panties. Her hands clutched at the back of my head to hold me captive against her generous mounds of flesh, and I was amazed at how susceptible they were to the efforts of my mouth. With nipples that sensitive, I figured, her clitoris should be absolutely explosive, and any stimulation of it would send her flying into space.

I had to test that theory. Wresting my head from her hold, I dropped to my knees and nudged her thighs apart. She nodded enthusiastically to that as she spread her legs wide, revealing the glistening pink petals of her pussy and her protruding clit. Her musky fragrance overwhelmed my senses; I breathed in her heady scent, taking a moment to appreciate her naked beauty. However, my attempt at patience was a failure. A split second later, I had my nose completely buried between her puffy labia and my lips were suctioned to her moist center. Quickly honing in on her swollen clit, I flicked my tongue against her button frantically. Fueled by my growing erotic hunger, I increased the intensity of my tongue-work and delighted in the flood of tangy juices that rewarded my efforts. She was just as worked up as I was, and I knew she wouldn't last long.

It seemed that I'd barely gotten started when Erin started shaking with bliss. I wasn't really surprised by that because her extreme arousal mirrored my own heightened state. My balls practically ached with the anticipation of being sucked. As I wrapped my lips around my partner's slick button and suckled it hard, I reached up to slide a finger into her hole. Her muscles clenched around my thrusting digit as her juices dripped down my wrist, and her slippery nubbin of flesh started pulsing wildly. Her body buckled, and then she let out a squeal and grasped my head.

I wrapped an arm around her waist and held her tightly as she quaked through an almost-violent orgasm. Then I endeavored to coax another series of small spasms out of her by using various tricks of my tongue, stopping only when Erin pulled me up onto the bed beside her and pushed me onto my back. Too impatient to take off my pants, she yanked down my fly and reached into my boxers to pull out my erection. She wrapped her fingers tightly around the base of my shaft and lowered her head to rewrap her lips around my bulbous crown.

My hips surged upward, but she pulled away, leaving my dick to bob forlornly in the air. As I chastised myself for my lack of control, Erin turned around and threw a leg across my torso. She was now crouching right above my head, her pussy hovering over my mouth, and her delicious slit was the last thing I saw as she lowered herself onto my face and again took my cock between her lips.

Desire surged through me, and I willed my ass to stay glued to the mattress so that she could continue doing her thing as her head descended over my length. I lapped at her labia softly, figuring that she'd still be sensitive from her climax, and thought about spinning her around to pierce her cunt with my cock. That consideration only lasted for about a second because she was sucking me with such relish that it seemed silly to make her stop. Besides, her pussy tasted amazing, so I redoubled my efforts upon it and began preparing us both to reach another climax.

I thrust my stiffened tongue into her juicy hole, eliciting a fresh flow of tangy juices from her slit. I gulped them down as Erin moaned around my shaft, once again setting her vocal chords to "vibrate." With my desperate prick buried halfway down her throat, my butt flew up off the bed, forcing her to swallow the remaining two or three inches. Taking it like a champ, she tightened her lips to hold onto me. I pulled back out, and then shoved back in, the tug of her mouth on my rod driving me even closer to release.

I managed to not lose my head, so I could continue my thorough tongue-fucking of Erin's cunt. Soon she was quaking so hard that I had to take hold of her asscheeks to keep her planted on my face. She began writhing so wildly that all I had to do was remain lying there as she got herself off—her body wriggling against my outstretched tongue did the rest. As she was overcome by her convulsions, her mouth ceased working but her throat muscles continued reverberating due to an incessant crescendo of moans. That's what finally tipped me over the edge of sanity, and I announced my release with a shout that was muffled in the fluttering petals of my partner's cunt.

Now at a full boil, the contents of my balls shot right through my shaft to explode from the head of my dick, sending a steady stream of cream over her tongue. As I served her my load, she kept gulping hard in a desperate attempt to swallow it all, and I'm still amazed by her fortitude, especially since she was riding the waves of her own orgasm at the time. Endeavoring to keep up, I continued swabbing her pussy until she grew too sensitive and released my cock from the vise-like grip of her lips and slid off my face to curl up at my feet.

I turned around to face her so that we could share a kiss that was filled with lots of tongue and redolent of our mixed flavors. The snow continued falling outside the windows of our hotel room as Erin started to snore softly beside me, and I hoped for another day of inclement weather to keep us stranded there. However, the storm had stopped by the next morning, the roads were all clear and our flight had been rescheduled to a time that didn't even leave us enough wiggle room for another quick sixty-nine.

I expressed my wistful disappointment as we repacked, and she smiled and squeezed my crotch. It turned out that while I'd been in the bathroom, she'd called the airline and had her seat switched so that we were sitting together. I shouldn't have been surprised; of course she'd find a way for us to have even more fun in the air, and we did, numerous times, before we landed. Although the last time I saw Erin was when we parted at the gate, I'll never be able to board a plane without thinking of her.

Exquisite Tastes

TAMMY SMALLS

"You have an oral fixation," my boyfriend, Josh, said from his position between my thighs.

"*I* have an oral fixation?" I repeated, feeling totally dumbfounded as I looked down at my handsome lover. I was so surprised by his offhanded comment because *he* was the one with the tantalizing tongue making those unbelievably sexy circles up and over my clit. He was the one whose fingers were spreading my bare pussy lips wide apart, creating that devastatingly sexy ache within me. And he was the one who was alternating those soft, sexy circles with gentle licks followed by delicate nibbles—three different sensations that had me nearly screaming in pleasure. With Josh touching me like that, every nerve ending of my body was tingling with sexual satisfaction.

"Yeah," he murmured sweetly against my tender skin, his soft hair rubbing against my thighs as he nodded his head. "You do, Tammy."

I couldn't believe what I was hearing, and although I knew this wasn't the most appropriate time or place for a disagreement, I couldn't stop myself from responding.

"Me?" I demanded, pushing myself up on my arms to gaze down at him. I knew my blue eyes were blazing. "But you're the one who's—" Yet I couldn't actually continue the conversation, because his tongue started right up again, flicking my clit and instantly rendering me speechless. He wasn't playing fair at all! As his magical tongue tricked along my swollen clit, I immediately lost the power to talk and think. He knew perfectly well what he was doing. There he was, labeling me as orally insatiable and then making it absolutely impossible for me to argue. It's probably one of his more underhanded lawyerly tactics, although I'm quite certain he doesn't employ this trick when making a case in a crowded courtroom—but wouldn't that be the ultimate crowd-pleaser?

As he continued to tease me, his tongue rotating in dangerous circles around and around my hot little button, I fell back into the luxurious pile of pillows at the head of our bed. I balled my hands into fists at my sides and started panting, my body shivering underneath him with barely restrained passion. Every inch of my skin was drenched in wicked wetness. My thighs were wet. The rumpled, pink satin sheets beneath me were wet. Josh's handsome face was wet. His sense of timing was unreal. The warmth of his tongue on my pussy had me quivering all over. The pressure of his mouth was divine—the way he'd touch my clit firmly and then back off to let me recover. Then again, there he was, touching me just so...

Perhaps he was right. Maybe I did have an oral fixation. I'd never really considered it before. Perhaps that's why I always keep hard candy in a jar on my desk in the office, something to pop into my mouth while I work all day. And I couldn't disagree that I often want to start our sex sessions on my knees in front of Josh, sucking him all the way to the root. Certainly, at that moment, I was most definitely fixated on him and the way he was orally pleasuring me.

Surrendering to my desires, I opened my fists and twisted my fingers in his thick hair, holding him to me, keeping him exactly where I needed him. I no longer wanted to continue our conversation. I didn't want to enter into what would surely become a lively debate, as such discussions with Josh always are. The only thing I knew for certain was that I wanted his tongue on me, taking me higher, taking me precisely where I needed to go.

But then, almost before I realized what was going on, I needed more. "Quick—" I begged, my hands slipping from his hair to his broad, tanned shoulders, my cranberry-colored fingernails dark against his skin. "Let me taste you."

"See, Tammy?" He was smiling. I knew he was smiling, even though I couldn't fully see his face because it was still pressed against my slit, since I felt the tickle of the corners of his lips curling upward against my flesh. "You like to have something in your mouth." There were more tickles as he spoke those words; I could feel them more than hear them. And I knew that he was right. At least, half right.

"Need," I corrected him, impatiently tossing my blonde curls out of my face so that my hair fell past my shoulders. "I *need* to have something in my mouth." I didn't have to tell him that he'd won.

His teasingly condescending tone of voice assured me that he knew it already. However, what he'd really won was more significant than the satisfaction of being right. He'd won the prize of my waiting, willing mouth. Luckily, he didn't seem to be in the mood to withhold what I wanted. With a low laugh, Josh quickly made my dreams come true. Maneuvering his lean body on the bed, he positioned his rock-hard cock directly in front of my waiting lips. I admired his fully erect shaft for a moment. His dick was long and thick, and just looking at it made me hunger for him even more. I gave his pulsing length one dramatic lick from top to bottom, and Josh groaned as he bucked his hips.

My hands automatically moved around his body so that I could be in control. I wanted to work him the way he'd worked me, tease him slowly, build him up in aching increments of pleasure. Josh had spent several minutes between my thighs, taking me higher and higher as though he was trying to find the answer to that age-old question: How many licks does it take…well, to make Tammy come? He had given me the most delicious sort of tongue bath any woman could ever desire, and he definitely deserved the same in return. He deserved all that and more. But suddenly Josh brought his warm mouth back down to my clit again, and every single thought fled my head. Clearly, he was intent on making me climax.

As he once again tripped the tip of his tongue around my clit, I felt the need to scream building within me. I wanted Josh's strong, hard cock between my lips while he used his tongue and fingers to pleasure my pussy. To my great satisfaction, my boyfriend didn't have any problem with the desires winging fiercely through me. Instinctively, he slid forward, pressing the rounded head of his cock against my full lower lip. As he slowly pushed his cock into my mouth, his fingertips began to probe my pussy.

"Oh yes," I mumbled around his shaft, letting him know that he'd given me exactly what I craved. One finger massaged my velvety insides, but soon one finger was not enough and I pulled my mouth off his shaft to let him know.

"Please," I begged him, the word coming out so breathy and full of desperation that he didn't need me to say anything else.

With ease, he overlapped two fingers and used them to fuck my slit, while keeping his mouth locked in place on my clit. I instantly returned my lips to his shiny cock, eager to pay him as much devoted oral attention.

I moaned, delighting in the scent of him, the rich taste of his warm skin, the hardness of his rod in my mouth, the veins pulsing and bulging prominently along his length. "More, Josh, more—" My words were delightfully slurred against the thickness of his cock, but Josh seemed to understand precisely what I was asking for.

He fucked my mouth, feeding me inch by rock-solid inch, his lips and fingers never leaving my pussy for a second. While I sucked him, his tongue continued playing X-rated games with my clit, raising my level of arousal higher and higher and bringing me closer to the point of no return. I stopped thinking about anything as I drank from him, my mouth caressing him, my body aching for release. I was certain that the warm, wet world of my mouth was pleasing him as much as his tongue on my pussy was pleasing me. I did my best to provide a steady, dependable rhythm for him, completely swallowing his length each time he thrust it into my mouth.

As I felt the climax building within me, I slammed against his body from below, doing my best to drive his fingers even farther into my pussy, desperate for deeper penetration. My mouth never wavered from his cock. I never let him slide all the way out, and I made sure to keep a trail of warm, wet saliva connecting my tongue to his cockhead. We were locked in a fabulous ring of pure sexual intensity, and when I started to come, I felt closer to Josh than I ever had before. We were melded together like one being, and he drank from me as I drank from him, our orgasms intensifying each from the other. As he came, thrusting firmly down my throat, I hungrily swallowed every single drop of his load as if it was the sweetest nectar on earth. His cream coated my throat as it slid all the way down, satisfying one part of my voracious hunger.

"Oh god," I sighed when he pulled out of my mouth. I felt momentarily emptied, saddened by the loss of his turgid flesh between my lips, wanting to suck on him forever. "Oh, Josh—"

He was as flushed as I was, his cheeks the same pinkish hue as when he's finished a morning run. I could have shut my eyes, curled my body around his and gone right to sleep in the glow of the sunbeams warming our bed, but Josh had entirely different plans. Thank god for that, because Josh's plans often lead to me having earth-shattering orgasms.

As soon as he caught his breath, Josh crawled up my body to give me a kiss that was richly redolent of my pussy juice. With our tongues entwined, my cunt tingled with a fresh hunger. He didn't speak, just continued lavishing me with kisses, sparking my desire yet again. Looking into Josh's dark-green eyes made me feel exposed, as if he could see inside me to my soul, into all of my secret fantasies. With Josh, that's a good thing. I want him to climb inside my mind and discover all of the dirty fantasies and desires that await him.

Josh left me reclining against the pillows and slid down my body, settling himself between my still-splayed legs. He pressed one of his thumbs against my clit and then brought his free hand up to my mouth. He pushed his thumb against my lower lip and instantly I started to suck on it. I did this without thinking, without realizing that once again I was indulging my oral side. I simply drew his warm thumb a bit deeper into the wetness of my mouth, closing my eyes as I sucked on him.

"Yes, that's it," Josh encouraged me. I continued to suck Josh as he used his other hand to spread my still-swollen, still-dripping pussy lips. He breathed gently on me, and I quivered and stopped sucking his thumb. He immediately pulled back from me and said, "Tammy, I want you to continue. No matter what I do, you keep going."

It took every effort I had to follow this instruction, but the reward I received was almost instantaneous. As I sucked on his thumb, he returned to licking my pussy. I soon realized, however, that he was paying attention to the way I sucked him. He was mimicking the rhythm of my choosing with his tongue on my twitching clit. That swollen nub was still so sensitive from my first orgasm that I could barely stand the pleasure. Even his breath on me was almost too much. So when he actually sucked my clit into his mouth again, pulling on it over and over, I thought I might literally shatter from ecstasy.

With these thoughts in my head, it's not surprising that once again, despite Josh's strict instruction, I forgot to do my job. I momentarily forgot to show him with my mouth what I wanted him to do with his. Instantly, all pleasure stopped. I opened my eyes to see Josh looking up at me, his emerald eyes glowering. For an instant, I was embarrassed, sorry for disappointing him. But then my own temper began to rise and an even better idea came to mind. Two could play his game.

Without a word of warning or a breath of explanation, I swiveled my body around so that I was facing his lower half, my pussy still within reach of his lips. Then I gripped his hardened shaft and brought it to my mouth, settling my lips on the tip. Josh groaned with pleasure. I performed a slow flicking motion over the head and sensitive underside and did my best to send Josh messages with each and every little lick. *See?* I was saying with the tip of my tongue. *I like it like this. A little swirl. A tiny circle.*

Josh immediately understood and followed suit. Soon, he and I were messaging back and forth to each other with the speed and frequency of IMs on the computer.

Suck harder, he told me by nearly devouring my clit.

Slow down, I replied with a restrained bob along the full length of his rod.

Tap your tongue gently on the tip, he begged.

Trace letters around my clit, I responded.

Touch me like this, we both demanded. *Touch me exactly like this!*

Our sexy game soon morphed into a pornographic version of Simon Says. We played using only our fingers, palms, lips and tongues, and when either one of us became too creative on his or her own, the other was quick to reply—*Ah, ah, ah! Simon didn't say that.* Of course, the entire conversation was conducted via oral actions, which made the encounter all the more erotic. I showed Josh with my body, with the way I wriggled in his arms or bucked closer to his mouth, that I reveled in his touch, in every lap of his curious tongue and kiss of his lips.

Josh thrust deeper, trying to pound into my throat each time I used my little finger to stroke behind his balls. We found ourselves listening intently to each other's cues and responding. When Josh's fingers caressed my ass, I responded in kind. When he pulled back and simply breathed on me, I did the same. We played this game of teasing each other until I was almost out of my mind. I felt giddy, dizzy, my body literally trembling. I was focused fully on giving Josh what he wanted, and he was acting the same way.

Almost too soon, I began to decipher the message that he was going to come. But this time, he added a clear verbal instruction. "Get on top of me, Tammy. I want to fuck you."

As soon as he spoke, I realized that I wanted that, too, and I quickly obeyed, sliding around again to face him, gliding my slick pussy down over his shaft and riding cowgirl-style as he bounced me up in the air with the motions and power of his energetic thrusts. Of course, my oral fixation didn't leave me for a second, and Josh knew that. But this time, he gripped my waist tightly and pulled me down so that we were kissing, his tongue probing my mouth as his cock filled me below. I lost myself in his kiss and the satisfaction of his radiant movements. Kissing and fucking soon gave way to coming, and I surrendered to the demolishing force of pleasure that exploded deep within me. Josh came a beat after me, and then held me tight to him with his muscular arms wrapped around my body as the reverberations of bliss echoed through us both.

As we lay there, Josh let his fingers wander along my cheekbones, tracing up and down and slowly moving lower until he brushed my lips, and I found myself licking his fingertips. Tasting salt, sweat and skin. Tasting Josh. Tasting myself. Josh chuckled at my automatic response, and I felt a blush rising in my cheeks. When I put my hand out, I felt something else rising as well. He was hard again, and I was as hungry as ever.

Orally fixated? Perhaps I am. But orally satisfied? Never.

Deep Hunger

Gary Holmes

Ah, the blow job. Breathes there a man who doesn't relish the sight and feel of his cock disappearing into a woman's warm mouth, putting himself completely under her control until he spills his creamy load down her sleek throat? I doubt it. For me, getting sucked off by a woman whose expertise matches her enthusiasm has always been a special pleasure. It wasn't until Arianne entered my life, however, that I discovered how extraordinarily pleasurable and satisfying a blow job could be when administered by a woman with an absolute passion for the act.

Arianne and I met when we were graduate students at a local college outside Miami. Everyone on campus thought of her as a real hot number. Raven haired, tanned and tall with a voluptuous body, she cut an impressive figure. Of French and Greek origins, fluent in not only those languages but also German and Italian, she lent a touch of class to our surroundings. She was working toward a master's in linguistics while I was studying comparative literature; our academic paths crossed in a seminar on Greek and Roman poetry entitled The Literature of Metamorphosis.

At the seminar table that first class, I could not take my eyes off her. When she spoke, I took in the way Arianne's breasts rose provocatively beneath her white V-neck T-shirt as her hands fluttered through the air, nervously but authoritatively underlining her points. Her mouth, lipsticked in coral, drew my attention, and I caught flashes of a fetching pink tongue dancing between her teeth, which left me spellbound.

The next evening, quite by chance, I ran into Arianne on the beach near where she lived. I'd just left a bar right as Arianne was saying good-bye to a friend on the street. It was a balmy night, and Arianne and I fell right in step with each other, walking in the direction of the beach, each happy to have the company. We sat down on a bench on the low-hung boardwalk and looked out to the sea.

It was a magical night. Arianne and I forgot that we'd only met for the first time the previous afternoon. She spoke about how the beach reminded her of her grandfather's house in the Greek Isles. She looked beautiful in the dim moonlight, and I told her so. She glanced away, then looked at me again with bold resolve. "Maybe the Romans were right," she finally responded. "The body does affect the mind. Since yesterday, I haven't been able to think about anything but being with you." I bent low and kissed her hand, breathing in the earthy scent of her flesh. "Please come home with me tonight," Arianne murmured.

We walked to her building with its white exterior that made me feel like we really could have been in the Greek Isles. Her cool, dimly lit apartment, swept by the odor of the sea, swallowed us up, and I forgot all about the outside world. Seating us on a black leather recliner, Arianne brushed her soft lips against mine, accepting my eager kisses. My hands roamed her body, and as I felt for the soft curves of her breasts, I could feel an unmistakable metamorphosis taking place in my cock. As Arianne's slender hands touched me, she noticed as well, and slid to her knees in front of me.

She lowered her head over my lap and kissed my ever-growing cock through my jeans. With her elegant hand, she unzipped my fly and drew out my cock, nuzzling it with her face, flicking her tongue over the shaft, feeling up and down its contour and length. Then she began to lick me in earnest, her dark, silky hair tumbling over my groin, obscuring my view of the actions of her mouth.

The sensation of having this beautiful woman's tongue, eager and wet, working its way up and down my cock was like nothing I'd ever felt before. I began to gratefully stroke her head. Sweeping back her hair with one hand, I could watch Arianne as she slipped her satiny lips over the head of my penis and nibbled at its top. Then she abruptly slid my entire cock into her velvety mouth, straining to swallow it whole. With her tongue working on the sides of my hard-on, and my shaft bulging in her mouth, Arianne sucked with wholehearted concentration. I exploded in a sudden violent burst, crying out her name as I came. She gulped down every drop of hot white cream my cock could generate as I grasped her shoulders through her silky blouse.

"Now, what would you like, Arianne?" I questioned, drawing her into my lap and pulling her toward me for a kiss.

"I'll have to think about that," she answered, "but we're going to have to wait for another time. You have to go now. I have an early class tomorrow."

From there, our relationship really took off. Arianne made it clear that she was a devotee of the blow job. Although her pussy—wet, pink and wondrously sensitive to the thrust of my penis—was certainly attractive, we fucked only rarely. It seemed as if we were enjoying oral sex more than regular intercourse. Arianne constantly amazed me as she led me through the pleasurable repertoire of her mouth; often I fingered her clit at the same time. Sometimes we'd end up entangled in a sixty-nine position, and I'd get a taste of her delicious pussy. I was happy to follow in whatever direction she led me.

One night we went out for dinner to a swanky restaurant. The food was spicy and the wine was plentiful, putting us both in a great mood. When we were finishing with some rich Spanish coffee and dessert, Arianne put down her cup without warning and requested to be taken home. Bewildered, I agreed, but understood her true motive when I saw the hungry look in her eyes. The urgency beneath her smile sent a signal to my groin, and immediately my cock was standing at attention. We quickly paid our bill and left. In the cab I tongued her ear and neck all the way home while she ran her fingers over my groin, kneading my balls and bringing my cock to an impossible hardness.

By the time we got upstairs, I was on fire. Arianne said she was going to change into something more comfortable, so I sat in the bedroom by myself, waiting for her to join me. When she finally entered the room, she was completely naked, her lithe legs smooth and dark, her ebony hair cascading down over her delightfully rounded breasts, her pussy peeping out from under a tuft of thick black hair. Her full red lips were parted, trembling in anticipation of receiving my hard-on.

"Was it worth the wait?" she cooed. Before I could answer she was on her knees, sweeping the hair back from her face, pulling down my fly and tenderly drawing out my stiffening member.

Kissing my penis once on the head, she then rubbed her breasts against my now-hard cock. Soon she brought her lips back down to my shaft and stroked it with her mouth, moving her head slowly from side to side. My cock grew larger, crowding her cheeks while she grasped my penis at the base as though she were trying to delay the flow of my come that was threatening to burst forth. Her efforts were in vain—it wasn't long before my cock surrendered to her mouth's onslaught, the smooth, white cream firing deep down her throat.

Playfully, Arianne let some of my come trickle over her lower lip, then looked up to let me see my seed streaming over her lips and chin. She looked beautiful, both submissive and dangerous at once. "I love listening to you moan," she purred warmly, her head resting on my thigh, the semen glistening on her lips as she spoke.

No two oral lovemaking sessions are ever the same with us. Sometimes Arianne sucks me long and hard, purposely prolonging the moment before she will let me come, releasing the pressure at just the second I am ready to burst. More often she wolfs me down, hungry and passionate, licking her lips to eat up every drop of my load. There was one particular morning, however, that stands out as being especially memorable.

I was fast asleep in Arianne's bed. At first I thought what I heard was the sea gently lapping at the bedroom walls, as though the apartment were a shell and I the oyster inside. As I began to slowly emerge from the cocoon of sleep, I became aware that the lapping was actually Arianne licking my balls, slowly and lovingly, her tongue pressing into the soft texture of my testicles and the already-hardened root of my cock.

"Good morning," Arianne murmured between strokes of that pussy-pink tongue I knew so well, a tongue that was now bringing me back to wakefulness and immediate passion. I opened my eyes and saw the ocean, barely lit by the newly risen sun, gleaming to the horizon outside the bedroom window. It was then that my lovely sea goddess enveloped my half-risen cock with her heavenly mouth. I looked down to see her sprawled over my groin in all her beauty, sucking on my rod, pressing it against the soft interior of her cheeks. Her hands slid under my ass, the nails digging into the skin that sloped toward my anus, forcing me to jerk up to escape her fingers and driving my cock farther into her mouth and down her moist throat.

Her whole head bobbed up and down as she rode my cock, her temperature rising so that she broke into a sweat. I felt my lava slowly rise, gradually gaining force as she expertly guided the intensity, stoking the fire but not yet letting it flame out of control.

Passion was still rising in me as she loosened her hands from my ass and for a few moments lovingly cupped my balls, kneeling over me in order to maneuver herself into the position she wanted. Her mouth remained on my cock as she situated herself so that her pussy was directly above my mouth. Breathing in her musky odor, I delighted in the luscious pink sex that was presenting itself to me, to do with as I liked. I darted my tongue out, taking a tentative taste as though this were a strange new treat and not Arianne's familiar cunt. Inspired, I began lapping along her folds, searching for her clit, which I knew was carefully hidden there. When I found her tender bud, it hardened underneath my tongue as she writhed and gasped above me.

I continued my actions on her pussy as she began to moan, her body bucking against mine. The vibrations from her mouth hummed against my cock, intensifying the sensations I was already feeling. We were caught in a cycle—our reactions spurring each other's actions, our moans mixing in the morning air, until finally it seemed as though our passion couldn't get any more intense. When I thought I couldn't take any more, Arianne cried out, her mouth slipping off my cock as her body succumbed to the sweet force of her orgasm.

Barely missing a beat, Arianne once again engulfed my cock with her mouth. She sucked me hungrily as her pussy quivered over my face with the last tremors of her climax. I was unable to hold back any longer and felt myself losing it. Arianne made me feel as if she were going to deep-throat all of me, eat me up, inside and out, until nothing was left and I was part of her. Our bodies shook under the force of our mutual pleasure. The beautiful morning light draped us in its warm glow as we found our way into each other's arms, drifting back into a deep sleep.

I never feel so sexy as when I am thinking about the way my darling Arianne pleasures me with her mouth, and I am always more than happy to return the favor. At the same time, I'm at her mercy when she holds my manhood between her teeth and makes me a part of herself. Graduate studies have turned out to be more rewarding than I ever expected, and I am learning as much out of the classroom as I am learning in it.

O *is for Orgasm*

SONIA CHOI

As dawn broke on the first day of our vacation, Jack woke me with a good-morning kiss. This wasn't your average smooch, lips pressed chastely together in a sweet display of love and affection. Instead, he burrowed under the soft mountain of blankets and spread my pussy lips open with his long fingers. The first rays of sunlight were dazzling on the white coverlet as Jack's body moved and wriggled underneath. I could feel his hot breath on my cunt the second before his lips made contact with my skin. That light puff of air made me tremble all over in a wave of delicious anticipation.

Jack started slowly, so that I teetered on the precipice of pleasure for the longest possible time. Making me wait for it, he slowly licked my inner thighs, teasing me until I begged. "Please, Jack. Lick me."

I sighed as he finally circled my clit with his full lips and bestowed a kiss that registered powerfully at the very center of my being. His tongue was wet and warm against my body, bringing forth my slick nectar. Jack had me completely soaked. After only a few French kisses to my clit, he slipped his tongue in and out of my cunt and then pressed it against me, awaiting my body's response. And, oh, did my body ever respond.

Closing my dark-blue eyes, I waited impatiently for what I expected would be the first climax of our vacation. But to my dismay, Jack suddenly stopped what he was doing and asked me a question.

"How does that feel, Sonia?" he murmured from underneath the bedcovers.

It felt good. So good, in fact, that I couldn't immediately make my mouth work to reply. "Don't you like it?" he asked when I didn't respond.

I knew from previous experience experiences with Jack that my dear husband wouldn't continue until I answered, and I managed to whisper, "Yes, baby."

"Tell me about it," he requested from beneath the sheets. Jack loves it when I talk dirty to him, but at that moment, I was speechless as his tongue and lips tickled against my skin. Desperate, I gripped his broad, muscular shoulders as my hips rose upward, pressing even harder against his hidden face. I could easily visualize the expression in his hazel eyes, the way he would be staring intently at my pussy.

"Come on, Sonia," he urged again. "Talk to me."

"Your tongue feels so good against my clit," I finally told him. Instantly, Jack rewarded my efforts, dipping his wriggling tongue between my dripping pussy lips to lick and lap like a hungry tomcat before drawing my juices back into his mouth. Of course, now that he'd given me a taste, I wanted him to continue kissing and licking my cunt until I came all over his mouth.

Unfortunately, Jack didn't do what I hoped. As soon as he realized how excited I was, he slid off the bed and disappeared into the bathroom. Dazed, I reached one hand between my legs and urgently stroked myself, trying to recapture the feeling he'd started, but failing. I needed his mouth, and I was thankful when he returned to the bed, resuming his position between my widespread thighs. Yet what I felt against my pussy surprised me so much that I sat up with a start.

A shocking icy blast had tingled all the way through me, and I quickly figured out what it was from both the scent and the sensation. Jack had used mouthwash, and the cool, mentholated fragrance lingered on his tongue. Slowly, I lay back down on the mattress, letting the sensations flood through me. It was a unique experience, icy yet hot, and I tossed back my head as Jack continued to work his magic. My long blonde hair feathered over the pillow, creating a silky curtain as I rocked back and forth.

Who would have thought that good oral hygiene could feel so fucking sexy? The minty sensation spread through my pussy, making my labia tingle and turning my clit into a hot zone. I felt like I was on fire as the warmth radiated through my body, spreading outward in delicious flickers.

"Oh, baby," I whispered. "Lick me harder. Make me come."

"Like this?" Jack asked, moving his mouth away long enough to speak before resuming those dreamy licks and nips. He set exactly the right pace, playing and teasing, letting the pleasure and the pressure build at a perfect rhythm.

"Yes," I sighed, "exactly like that."

He gave me a little more. His tongue probed me, tricked along my lips and then slid inside my cunt. He used his hands to keep my body steady, my hips resting gently in his large, steady palms. As I started grinding against him, he upped the intensity, licking harder and firmer along the seam of my body until I thought I couldn't take any more. I knew that in moments I would come with the ferocity of a Fourth of July firecracker, with explosions that would rocket through both my husband and myself. But once again, Jack surprised me. Sliding up on the bed, he maneuvered his body so that he could enter me with his large and ready hard-on.

To have his cock inside me after his tongue had gotten me all warm and wet was the ultimate erotic feeling. I started squeezing him instantly, my pussy contracting like a powerful fist around his rock-hard shaft, making him moan with the enthusiasm of my body's response. Jack's thick cock, with its bulbous tip, plunged into me. As I squeezed him, he thrust harder into me, slamming against my body until his balls met my skin.

"Fuck me, baby," I said, staring into his eyes and taking in the glossy wetness that lingered around his mouth, wetness that had come from my body. "And kiss me," I added, hesitating before saying, "so I can taste my juice on your lips."

Those words were just dirty enough to make Jack moan, and he leaned forward to stare deeply into my eyes as he pumped me. Then he did as I'd asked, bringing his mouth to mine, parting my lips with his tongue. We shared a kiss flavored by both the minty-freshness of the mouthwash and the sweet muskiness of my own juices. The combination was so sexy that it finally made me climax. My contractions swelled dramatically from deep within my body, bringing him right up to the edge along with me.

"Oh fuck," he moaned, biting onto my bottom lip as he came. "Oh, Sonia." He shot his load inside me and then stayed sealed to my body, before finally pulling his spent cock from my pussy.

We took a much needed and well-deserved break then, sprawled lazily on the rumpled bedclothes, both of us trying to regain our sense of balance. After several minutes, Jack started discussing our plans for the day. He thought we might go sightseeing since we were, after all, on vacation. There were beaches to walk along, surf to tiptoe through. We had snorkeling junkets to book, mai tais to drink. But I had other ideas, and I relaxed against the pillows and whispered, "Baby, are you thirsty?" I used a coy expression of mine that always lets him know that I have some kinky treat in store for him.

"Thirsty?" Jack asked, wondering what I was planning. "For what?"

"There's an ice machine down the hall," I said suggestively. "Why don't you go and fill us up a bucket."

Without another word, Jack slid into one of the plush white terry-cloth robes kindly provided by the hotel and went on his mission for ice. I heard the chips clinking in the plastic bucket, and I grinned as Jack opened the door and brought the ice to the bed. Now it was my turn to play.

As Jack watched intently, I took a chip of ice and sucked until my mouth was nice and cold. Then I told him to roll over so that he was on his stomach, facedown on the bed. He gave me a quizzical look but then obeyed, rolling over on the mattress and putting his hands over his head to hold onto the bars of the metal headboard. I didn't have to tell him to do that. He guessed without my help that he would need something to hold onto in order to keep himself still.

For a few lust-filled seconds I paused to observe my husband's delicious body. He is tall and well built, with tanned skin the color of freshly baked gingerbread. His hair is a slightly darker shade of brown, like milk chocolate, and he wears it long, so that I have something to run my fingers through. But on this morning, I wasn't concerned with his attractive face, his sculptured jaw or the lines of the muscles that run along his back. No, where I wanted to spend some time was with his lower region, the twin mounds of his firm, round ass.

As I admired Jack, I gently played my fingertips along his asscheeks until he moaned. It was obvious to me that he didn't know what I was going to do next, and that slight apprehension was extremely arousing to him. I let him wonder for a few moments more because I could tell that what he didn't know was making him hard.

Finally, with a gentle motion, I cupped his cheeks in my hands and spread them wide apart, disclosing his little pink anus. The sight of it made me damp all over again. Then I wet the tip of my pinkie and tickled the rim of his hole, skating my cool fingertip around and around. Jack moaned and shifted on the bed as I parted his cheeks as wide as I could. Then I bent, and with my still-icy tongue in a point, ran it around his tiny rosebud.

"Oh fuck, that's cold," he said.

"But you like it?" I asked as I reached for another ice chip.

In response, Jack groaned and lifted his hips. I sucked on a piece of ice until it had practically frozen the tip of my tongue, then I resumed my oral activities. I continued flicking my tongue over his quivering asshole as he groaned and clutched the headboard a little more tightly.

"That is so fucking dirty," Jack said into the pillows. "Don't stop."

I wasn't about to stop. Instead, I slipped one hand under his hips and held onto his shaft, jerking it firmly while I pressed my face deeper between his cheeks. I could feel his cockhead getting wet again, his precome making his erection slick and difficult to grasp. And as I pumped Jack's dick, I traced designs over his asshole with my tongue, exactly like he does when he's eating my cunt. But I could tell it wasn't enough; my husband wanted more.

Moving back, I wet two of my fingers in my mouth and slowly pushed those into his asshole. With one hand, I kept his cheeks spread wide. Then I started gently fucking him with my hand, plunging in deep and withdrawing. Jack helped, humping the mattress as I finger-fucked him until he simply couldn't take the sensations anymore. At least, that's what he thought. As he approached his limit for the second time that morning, I put a third finger into his hole, filling his velvety tunnel. I was so turned on that I had to reach down and stroke myself with my free hand. Just as I was about to climax, Jack told me to stop.

"Sonia, hold it," he said, his voice a harsh whisper. What he really meant was "let go," because he wanted us in a sixty-nine. Quickly. "I want to come in your mouth," he said breathlessly.

I did as he said, sliding next to him on the mattress head-to-tail as he rolled onto his side. He immediately grabbed my slender hips and pulled me toward his mouth, introducing his tongue to my clit for the second time of the morning. My cunt felt relaxed and ready for round two. In fact, I could imagine spending all day—all weekend, even—in bed with my husband, fucking until we could no longer talk or walk.

I parted my lips and welcomed his cock down my throat. But

even as I sucked him hungrily, I played my fingertips along the crack of his ass, stroking and strumming him toward a body-tingling, bed-shaking orgasm. And as Jack approached his orgasm, he didn't forget about me—or my needs. In fact, the hotter he got, the more carefully he worked me, taking me on one of my most favorite trips of all.

My husband likes to trace the letters of the alphabet over my clit, all the way from *A* to *Z*. He takes his time, as if he's going to be graded on penmanship, and I generally come by *L*, if not sooner. Sometimes he even hums the *ABC* song simultaneously, and the vibra-tions flow through my body, thrilling me from the inside out.

As I sucked him that morning, he began his *ABC* game. Yet as I was getting into the groove, he stopped at *D*, wanting to change positions again so that I was on my back and he was poised above me. I got a good look at Jack's cock, which was turning purplish at the head, before taking it back in my mouth. I had to reach up for it—my body straining, my lips open for his thick, swollen prick. Usually, I adore stroking his sensitive skin with my tongue before pulling his dick into my mouth, but now I wanted to get right to it, wanted to feel the head pounding against the back of my throat.

Jack would not be rushed. Moving slowly, he teased us both, dipping his cock into my mouth for one long beat before pulling out and rubbing himself along my lips and cheeks so that they were wet and shiny. I opened my mouth, waiting for him to plunge in again, but instead, he shifted his body so that his balls were poised over my open lips. Then he leaned forward, dunking them in my mouth. I sucked gently, losing myself in his scent. I could have spent hours in that position, going back and forth between caressing his balls with my tongue and then slurping his powerful cock.

While I played with him, Jack continued the game with his tongue against my pussy. Now that we were in sync, he resumed his *ABC* routine. And as usual, by the time he was halfway through the alphabet, I had reached my peak, bucking against his mouth during *L, M, N, O* and *P,* coming on his lips and sucking his cock even harder, taking him down to the root. Groaning into my pussy, he shot his load as my own climax continued flowing through me. I could feel his thick white cream spurting against my tongue and trickling down my throat.

We were silent for a few seconds, especially since I had to swallow. Then Jack swiveled around so that we were facing the same direction, and he took me into his arms. He didn't seem to care that we were both drenched with sex juices and sweat. Jack looked at me and said, "You're beautiful, Sonia." He hugged me tightly as I thought that this was the perfect way to start our vacation.

Dinner for Two

DANA TRAVIS

"Hey, baby, what's cooking?" Todd called out as he entered our house. This is his standard question on the nights when I make it home from work before he does. We often take turns preparing meals for each other, each of us delighting in the surprise of a waiting feast. This evening, however, the kitchen was closed, and Todd had to pass through the swinging wooden doors and into the dining room to find me.

The gilded light of glimmering candles momentarily shocked him into stunned silence. He blinked curiously at the sight spread out before him on our table. My favorite heavy lace tablecloth dressed up the sturdy antique table, and an extravagant bouquet of fragrant white roses sat on the nearby credenza. All that was lacking from the well-planned decor was the silverware, napkins, glasses and plates. But that was okay. We weren't going to need any of those things for the dinner I had planned.

"Did I forget something, Dana?" he asked, sounding concerned. "Are we expecting company?"

"I had a good day at work," I told him, smiling. "We're celebrating."

"But what are we eating?" he asked, looking even more bewildered. I answered his question with actions rather than words, and his eyes widened in surprise. In one slinky gesture, I pulled my lavender dress over my head and tossed it onto a chair. As Todd gazed at me, I brought my hands between my breasts and unsnapped the clasp of my frilly white bra. This piece of luxurious lingerie perfectly matched the lace of the tablecloth, which was intentional on my part. I'd planned the evening down to the tiniest detail, going so far as to coordinate my outfit with the formal table linens.

With Todd's eyes still focused intently on my every move, I let down my long hair, removing the pins in the back and shaking my dark tresses free. Then I reached for the final touch to my outfit, which was hanging on a nearby chair. It was a dainty, see-through apron, and I fastened it around my waist so that the ties of the bow hung down loosely in the back. Clad only in my apron, panties, garter belt with fishnet stockings and insanely high-heeled stilettos, I struck a sexy pose for my husband and waited for his response.

A charming smile lit up his eyes, but he didn't move. He seemed to comprehend that something unique was going on and that if he let me lead the way, he would definitely enjoy himself. As he stared at me, I stroked my breasts lightly, rubbing my palms in generous circles over my pink nipples. The rest of my body responded immediately, a sexy wetness developing beneath the apron, dripping from my pussy and drenching my panties. I shifted my hips from side to side, rubbing my thighs together to feel the warm moisture gathering between my legs.

"Oh, you bad girl," Todd said softly, his voice sounding low and husky. "Dana, just look at you."

At his words, I gazed at my reflection in the glass doors of our breakfront. My flowing black hair complemented my pale skin, and I felt a flush of heat flaming my cheeks. Desire beat fiercely in my expression.

I tweaked my nipples firmly between my fingertips, feeling them grow even more erect than they had been. Then I slowly licked two of my fingertips and traced that lush wetness in circles around those hardened nubs.

"Don't stop, Dana," Todd sighed. "Don't stop." As he spoke, he took a step forward, as if he wanted to take over for me and touch me with his own fingers or mouth, but I shook my head sternly.

"You wait your turn," I told him.

I reached under the apron and peeled my sticky panties away from my pussy, rolling them down my thighs and then kicking them off. The twin apron strings tickled the bare, peach-split crack of my ass, adding an extra naughty charge to my desire. I was dripping wet already, and the evening's festivities had barely gotten underway. I wondered if he could make out my scent from where he stood. From the ravenous look on his handsome face, I guessed that he could and that he found the heady aroma even more enticing than that of a home-cooked meal.

Standing in front of him again, wearing only that wicked apron, garter belt, stockings and spiked heels, I asked one simple question, "Are you hungry, baby?" He nodded quickly, as though saying a single word would dissolve the erotic vision before him.

"I'm so glad," I said, "because tonight I have prepared a special meal for you. In fact, it's a house favorite." I hoisted myself up onto the dining room table and spread my body out in front of him in a decadent display. The fancy lace beneath my ass created a cushioning layer on top of the hard, cold wood. "I hope you're ready," I continued, staring into his lust-filled eyes, "because your dinner has just been served."

"You mean my 'Dana,' don't you?" he asked, smiling. It was obvious to me that Todd's appetite had switched from a hunger for food to an urgent need for me. He took a step closer and then paused, as if he was unsure of what to do next. It seemed like he couldn't decide whether to take the time to strip out of his suit or simply bury his head between my spread thighs. Before I could offer my own selfish suggestion, he made the correct decision himself.

Walking to the edge of the table, he scooped up my round asscheeks in his hands and lifted my sopping pussy to his mouth. At first, he ate me through the transparent fabric of the apron, remembering how much I like the feeling of a barrier at the onset of stimulation. Todd's mouth played delightful tricks against the sheer material. I moaned when he traced the cleft between my pussy lips with his tongue. Licking hard, he connected with my fabric-covered clit in a jolt of wet heat, sending a shiver all through my body. Then Todd untied the apron, yanked it off me and got down to business. His tongue slipped between my swollen pussy lips, testing the wetness within my sex. He sighed when he realized how drenched I was, and then lapped energetically at my cunt, tasting me, sipping me, drinking my juices before driving his tongue deep inside me.

"I don't know whether to eat you or fuck you," he murmured into my dripping-wet slit.

"Both," I told him, urgently. "Both."

"Yes," he sighed, before pressing his tongue hard against my pussy again. Lapping at me hungrily, he made sure that I was nice and creamy before setting my hips gently back down on the table's edge. Then he ripped open his pants, not even bothering to take them off, and brought out his throbbing cock. With his gleaming eyes focused on mine, he slid his cockhead into my pussy. "Eat and then fuck. Fuck and then eat," he said, like a mantra. "That's what you want, baby, isn't it?"

Yes, that's exactly what I wanted. The feeling of being instantly filled was overwhelming. His cock pushed between the slippery walls of my throbbing pussy, driving into me hard and deep. I couldn't remember ever wanting him so badly, but the next moment, he was withdrawing from my cunt. It was as if he knew how much I could take before I'd go over the edge.

"Eat again," he said in his abbreviated manner, bending before the table to flick his tongue rapidly over my dripping pussy. The short ride to heaven he'd given me on his cock had made me even wetter than before, and he eagerly slurped up my juice.

"You're absolutely delectable," he whispered, just loud enough for me to hear him. The echo of his words vibrated against my pussy, making my clit twitch with pleasure. "I could eat you all night." I closed my eyes, more than ready to let him. His questing tongue seemed to disappear all the way inside my slit, until his mouth was firmly sealed against my pussy. Then he wriggled his tongue back and forth inside me, and I grabbed fistfuls of his hair with both hands and slammed myself against him.

As I bucked my hips toward Todd's face, he switched positions, keeping me teetering on the brink of ecstasy but not letting me reach my goal. I was so hot and ready, and my pussy was swimming in a pool of slippery nectar. I wanted to come, and Todd knew it. When all I needed was one more direct stroke of his tongue to my clit, he made loopy circles around it instead, torturing me sweetly, never even accidentally brushing against that hot gem.

"Please," I begged.

"Shh, sweetheart," he admonished me. "I'm eating."

He was teasing me with my own game, giving me a pussy-licking to outlast all others. As he continued to make those taunting circles around my clit, I got so excited that I thought I might literally combust if he didn't let me climax soon. I saw it clearly in my mind—I would flambé like cherries jubilee!

"Todd," I murmured.

"You're really ready, huh?" he finally whispered. My eyes were clenched shut, my whole body shuddering, desperately on the verge of climax. Before I could answer, he moved away from the table and reintroduced his cock into my cunt.

Going back and forth between feeling his tongue on my pussy and being pierced by his cock was sexual overload. What did I truly want? His tongue or his cock? I didn't know. I wanted them both. It was like being presented with a detailed menu at a fabulous restaurant. My mind reeled with choices. Did I want him to climb on top of me and shake the table with his powerful thrusts? Would I rather he flip me over and take me doggie-style? Perhaps I'd prefer we move into a sixty-nine so my mouth would have something to suck as I melted into the bliss of being dined upon? I could no longer think about what I wanted. I put myself in my husband's capable hands and let him choose the order of our courses.

He answered by pumping hard with his hips, and when he withdrew, a fresh flood of honey seeped from my pussy. But before offering me the pleasure of his tongue again, he stripped entirely out of his suit, letting me see his hard, muscled body glistening with sweat in the candlelight.

"Get ready, Dana," he murmured, staring down at me as he thrust his cock all the way into my cunt. Seconds later, he was back between my legs, his tongue playing those dreamy tricks along my dripping-wet pussy lips. He licked and nibbled each one in turn, teasing them before moving down to leave wet kisses on my thighs. Taking his time, he worked back up to the entrance to my pussy. He used his fingers to spread my labia wide open, and then he finally finished me off. Licking in sweet, satiny circles around my pulsing clit, he increased the pace and pressure until finally, I was coming. I threaded my fingers through his soft hair, searching for something to steady myself, as pockets of pleasure bubbled up and exploded inside me.

As I writhed through my release, Todd moved away from my pussy long enough to say, "I hope you enjoyed the first course, mademoiselle."

I stared up at the wood beams in our ceiling, trying to get myself under control. My body was still trembling, my heart racing. First course? That meant there would be a second course, possibly a third and most likely some sort of outrageous, indecent dessert. Before I could contemplate how Todd had managed to turn the tables on me, so to speak, he was pushing me up farther onto the table and then maneuvering us into a sixty-nine position.

I took a few seconds to admire the bulging, rose-colored head of his cock—so deep, so rich, so ready for my tongue to lick and flick over the tip—before I drew it and the rod deep down into my throat.

Without another moment of hesitation, I rewarded my husband for being such a good pussy-eater. I gave the head of his cock a deeply welcoming French kiss, getting it all slick and wet with the moist heat of my mouth. I tasted my tangy juices on him, and that made me incredibly hot. There is nothing more erotic to me than sucking my own flavor off of my husband's shaft, thinking about how his cock was just buried inside me.

My thoughts took a sharp detour when Todd returned his mouth to my pussy. He took his time, teasing me with his tongue as he tasted the ambrosial liquid of my orgasm. He knows to touch me softly after I climax, and he did exactly that, using whisper-soft caresses along the length of my tender pussy lips. I responded in kind, running my tongue up and down his throbbing shaft. As soon as we were in sync, Todd pursed his lips around my clit and gave it a firm suck.

Immediately, I mimicked his actions with my lips, closing them around his cockhead and treating it like a big, round lollipop. Todd moaned and bucked his hips against me. For several minutes, he had been choreographing our little dance, but now I was in charge again. Drawing the length of his cock all the way into my mouth, I swallowed around him. The tight contractions in my throat around his steel-like shaft made him moan even louder.

Pleased with the response, I kept feasting on him in my own style. I moved my mouth up and down, releasing a few inches of his cock before enveloping him once again. The shaft grew glossy with the wetness of my saliva, and Todd helped me find the pace that he most craved. Moving his hips, he arched against me, driving his cock in deep. Back and forth he went, thrusting in and then sliding out of my mouth, and never ceasing his tongue's caress of my pussy. The entire time I worked him, he treated me to a deliciously sensuous second course. But I was suddenly overwhelmed with greedy thoughts, envisioning myself coming again. I pressed hard against his face to gain the clit-to-tongue contact that would take me over the edge.

We played each other perfectly, using the experience of our years together to guide us. We moved in a sexy dance on the table until I was moaning around his dick, letting him know that I was going to come again. I continued to suck on him as my orgasm rose up and then crested in a wave of pleasure. A hard suck, a long swallow and then he came with me, quickly filling my mouth with his semen. I made sure to capture every delicious drop, so I would be able to swallow his whole creamy load.

"So, Dana," Todd started, rolling over and moving his body so that we were face-to-face. He grasped my waist with one strong arm and held me close to him. "What's for dinner?"

Now whenever I hear this question, once a simple query, my face blushes hotly and my pussy quivers. Those innocent words make me want to take my panties down and press my sex against my husband's handsome face, no matter where we are. I always choose the items on our erotic menu—pussy-licking, sixty-nining, come-swallowing—over food. And when we finish the first course, I wait on the very edge of my seat for course number two, and sometimes there's even room for dessert.

The Sky's the Limit

BETHANY FISCHER

My husband has always planned rather spectacular surprises for my birthday. The first year we were married, he picked me up from work and whisked me away to a romantic weekend at Niagara Falls. Last year, he planned a huge party and invited just about everyone I'd ever known. But my favorite thing about these celebrations is that they always end with some great oral sex—against a fence in the dark with the rushing of the falls behind us, or in the bathroom of the catering hall he'd rented for the party with the voices of our friends dangerously close.

This year, however, I was turning thirty, and wasn't quite as excited as I'd been in the past. In fact, when the alarm went off, I hit the snooze button and hid my head under the pillow. Then Jeff spooned against my back, and I cuddled against him.

"Happy birthday, Bethany," he whispered in my ear. I grumbled something about it not being happy at all, and he chuckled. Then he kissed the back of my neck, and I felt his lips working their way down my body.

I moved away. "I have to go to work."

He caught me and playfully held me tight. "Not today."

"It's Wednesday, and I didn't call in."

"I did it for you," he whispered and nibbled at my neck.

Immediately, my stomach clenched with nervousness. "You didn't plan some big surprise, did you? I wanted to have a quiet day."

"Perfectly quiet," he assured me, sliding lower. "Well, maybe not too quiet," he added before disappearing below the sheets to take his place between my spread legs.

Jeff has always been a connoisseur of oral sex, and I sighed as he parted my legs. His hot breath tickled the sides of my thighs, and his hands came up and squeezed my hard nipples between his fingers. I moaned as a surge of heat shot straight to my cunt. "Mmm," he murmured and breathed in deeply. "I can tell how much you want me." He licked a path up my thigh, eventually stealing a taste of my swollen outer lips. "Tell me exactly what you want."

I arched my back, pressing my tits against his hands. "I want your tongue on me," I said.

"Where?" he asked playfully.

I paused as he gently pinched my nipples between his fingers. "On my pussy," I managed to utter.

"Here?" he asked and flicked his tongue once between my dripping hole and my swollen clit.

"Yeah," I breathed and bucked my hips against his face.

But Jeff was a master of delicious torment. "Or here?" He flicked his tongue between my slit and my asshole.

I sighed in response. My pussy was hot and throbbing by this time, and though his fingers on my nipples felt amazing, it was no longer enough. I thrust toward him, and he chuckled. He licked up my thigh once more, barely touching my cunt with his tongue, then he gave the same attention to my other leg.

"Please, Jeff," I whispered to him.

"Please, what?"

"Fuck me with your tongue."

He groaned. For all his supposed control, I knew I could make him lose it at any second with a few dirty words. I gripped handfuls of the sheets as Jeff pushed my legs wide apart and stuffed his stiff tongue into my slit. Groaning, I thrust against him, and he strained to press as far into my body as possible.

Jeff teased me like that for a while longer, licking the length of my cunt and lapping up my freely flowing juices, and then he reached my sensitive clit.

This is where my husband's talent really shines. He licked gently up one side of my pussy, barely touching me with the tip of his tongue. My cunt throbbed in response. He did the same to the other side, and I trembled and felt his tongue's effects in every nerve in my body. Then, very gently, he licked up to my clit, withdrawing as he reached that most sensitive nub.

My senses screamed, and my pussy dripped. "Please, Jeff," I begged.

His tongue dipped lower and smeared my juices around, then he returned to my clit. This time there was no teasing as he frantically flicked my sensitive nub. His movements alternated between slow touches and rapid taps, all of which were driving me crazy with lust.

I was moaning and panting so hard that it felt as if all the blood had rushed out of my head, creating a hazy, surreal feeling. My body floated as my husband continued his oral assault on my cunt. My moans lengthened and intensified. Jeff knew I was ready to climax, and he continued to tongue me steadily and rapidly.

I bucked wildly against his face, and when I came, it was with a series of cries and shudders. Jeff didn't stop sucking me until he'd lapped up every bit of juice from my quivering slit. Then he held me for at least ten minutes afterward, until my body had recovered from the surge of desire and release. But it wasn't long before my limbs lost their heaviness, and my hand snaked down my husband's muscular chest and stomach.

Jeff isn't the only one who enjoys imparting oral pleasures, and he isn't the only one who's honed the skill to an art form. My fingers played at the line of hair above his thick cock. And although I came close, I never quite touched his throbbing shaft. He thrust his hips slightly, and his cock bobbed against the back of my hand.

"Patience, patience," I chided him.

I dipped my head lower and caught his nipple between my teeth. His groan was low and tortured as I slid my hand down his thigh, then brought it up below his sac, touching him with the backs of my fingers.

"Fuck, Bethany," he groaned. It was the closest he'd come to begging, and it was good enough for me.

I grasped his cock in my fist and began to lightly pump it up and down. Looking up at his face, I found him staring down at me with dark, lust-filled eyes.

"Do you like that, baby?" I asked.

He nodded, wrapped a handful of my long red hair around his fist and yanked me up to his mouth. His kiss was anything but gentle. His teeth clashed with mine, his tongue thrusting between my lips.

I moaned, and his mouth swallowed the sound. Then I broke away. My passion had been completely restored, and I slid down his body eagerly, kissing, licking and sucking as I went. By the time I reached his cock, I could barely wait to take him into my mouth.

I started slowly, merely tasting his cockhead, licking lightly around the rim. Then I licked up and down his shaft. He let out a long, slow moan as I settled in.

I worked my way down to his balls and took one in my mouth, rolling it gently with my tongue. Jeff's breath hissed through his teeth as I gave the other the same attention. By the time I'd worked my way back up to the tip, his dick was like a pillar of smooth, hot steel. I took his entire length in my mouth and sighed with pleasure.

With his hands lightly threaded through my hair, he lay still and allowed me to develop my own rhythm. I held the base of his shaft with one hand and began pumping my mouth up and down. I swallowed his hot, slippery cock until it bumped against the back of my throat, then drew back until the head almost popped out. I squeezed my lips together tightly as I moved. Jeff always says my mouth is as snug as any pussy.

It wasn't long before his slow moans changed to ragged breaths and his loose grip of my hair became a bit more intense. He met me thrust for thrust as his groans deepened, and while I continued the steady movement of my mouth, I reached down and massaged his balls. He let out one thunderous growl and then shot his come down my throat.

I swallowed eagerly, drinking him dry, but a dribble escaped and ran down my chin. As I sat up, I deliberately licked it all up.

"You're amazing, baby. Do you know that?" I smiled broadly, straddled his still-hard cock and impaled myself on its length. Then I rode him to a fast, satisfying peak.

We spent the rest of the day in bed, sucking and fucking, stopping only to take a break for lunch. By midafternoon, I'd decided that this was pretty much the best birthday I could have had. Quiet, with only my husband to share it. So I went down on him again to show my appreciation.

After he'd eaten me in return and I was lying with my head on his stomach, Jeff nudged me to get up.

"We have to go," he said. "You don't want to miss your surprise."

I figured his surprise was dinner at a fancy restaurant. "Can't we just stay here? We can order in…eat in bed." My pussy tingled at the thought of what kind of eating I actually had in mind.

Jeff just shook his head and slid out from under me. "We can eat here when we get back."

I frowned. "But I wanted to spend a quiet day alone with you."

"This will be quiet, I promise. And we'll be alone." He pulled on a pair of jeans and a shirt. "Well, almost alone. But I promise you'll enjoy it."

I was skeptical, but didn't want to seem unappreciative, so I took his cue and dressed in a pair of jeans and a blouse. Jeff came up behind me and rubbed my tits. "Not that I want to cover up this beautiful body," he said, "but you might want to wear a jacket."

"We'll be outside?"

"All I can tell you is you'll probably be glad that you did."

We climbed in the car, but no matter how much I questioned him, Jeff would not give me any answers. I finally stopped long enough to realize we were driving toward the country. After another few minutes, we rounded the knob of a hill. A large, flat field stretched before us, and in the middle of that field was a hot-air balloon.

It looked gorgeous in the waning sunlight, and I gasped.

"I thought you'd like it," Jeff said, unable to conceal his smile, as we parked our car near the edge of the field.

Together we walked toward the balloon, and by the time we reached our destination, the pilot was ready to go. We stepped into the basket, and with a mighty whoosh, the balloon began to climb higher and higher.

Our pilot smiled at me and gestured toward a picnic basket near my feet that contained a bottle of champagne and two flutes. "Happy birthday," he said, then turned away.

As my husband poured us each a glass of bubbly, I sighed. "This is perfect."

"So I was right? You like it?"

I took a sip from the flute he had handed me and nodded energetically. "It's the best present I can think of."

As I finished my champagne, I looked out at the beautiful scenery below us. The sun had begun to set and cast a pink glow over the landscape. Jeff took my empty glass and placed it in the basket. Then he pulled me back against his chest and began caressing my breasts through my jacket. "Care to make this interesting?" he asked.

I looked back at him, and he slipped his hands under both my jacket and shirt and rolled my nipples between his thumbs and fore-fingers. As the heat surged to my pussy, I whimpered softly and let my head fall against his shoulder.

His hands felt amazing on my tits, and I pressed my ass against his cock. Then I glanced back at our pilot. He wasn't looking at us, but I knew he could hear every word we said. "We're not alone," I said to Jeff.

"I took care of it," he replied. "He won't tell a soul."

The idea of Jeff eating me while another man stood not three feet away was incredibly exciting. Then my husband spun me around, leaned down and captured one erect nipple between his teeth, teasing it through the fabric of my shirt. He tugged slightly, and a gasp of pleasure escaped my lips.

My pussy throbbed so violently that I thought I might come right away. Jeff gave the same exquisite attention to my other nipple before he began to work at the button and zipper of my jeans. I helped him slide the material over my slim hips and stepped out of one leg.

Running his fingers over the folds of my pussy, Jeff teased the slick, hot flesh. I sighed in pleasure as we floated high in the air. Then he placed my foot on his shoulder, spread my swollen cunt lips apart and shoved his stiff tongue deep into my slit.

Words cannot begin to express the awesomeness of that moment. I gripped the edge of the basket and let myself soar. Jeff's tongue moved from my hole to my engorged clit and flicked the nub mercilessly. I bit down hard on my lower lip, and my cries escaped as hysterical whimpers.

The sun continued its descent, and my husband continued his slippery assault on my cunt. Before long I was shuddering, bucking my hips wildly as I thrust against his drenched chin and mouth. My pleasure was rising higher and higher, and I couldn't hold my cries in any longer. With one great moan of ecstasy, my climax overtook me.

I quickly dressed, and then Jeff held me close to him as my breathing returned to normal. Meanwhile, I snuck a glance at our pilot. He had his back to us, seemingly unaware of our shenanigans. Of course, I knew better.

"Happy birthday, baby," Jeff whispered. And indeed it was.

We spent a long, quiet moment looking out at the beautiful scenery below us. It was so peaceful to be floating above the world. But unable to resist, I soon slid my hand to my husband's bulging crotch. He exhaled sharply at my touch and pressed against my palm.

Jeff gripped the edge of the basket as I worked my way down his body and pulled his pants down his hard, lean thighs. In no time, I'd freed his cock and was stroking it lightly while I cupped his balls in my other hand. His pulse raced beneath my fingers.

The breeze ruffled my hair as we dipped slightly in the wind. I took Jeff's dick in my mouth, giddy with the knowledge that the people on the ground could see the balloon but had no idea what we were doing.

I rolled my tongue around the rim of my husband's cock, then took the entire shaft into my mouth and swallowed it down. Jeff loves it when I deep-throat him, and just like he had that morning, he threaded his fingers through my hair.

I worked him in and out, ramming the head of his cock against the back of my throat on each downward stroke. My mouth was everywhere—licking, sucking, biting—and I pumped his shaft furiously, needing to taste his cream.

Jeff let out a groan through clenched teeth, and I continued working him. Then he shot his load into me, and as he spurted, I swallowed eagerly, sucking every drop out of him. Then I gently licked him clean as he grasped the edge of the basket to maintain his balance. Pulling his pants up over his legs, I slid back up his body.

As we floated above the unsuspecting world, I leaned close to my husband. "This is unquestionably the best birthday I've ever had," I said happily. We kissed deeply, and I knew that he had enjoyed it, too. It seemed that turning thirty wouldn't be as bad as I had thought!

Mouth to Mouth

Elisa Nolan

My legs were bent, feet tucked back so far that my heels practically touched my asscheeks. I kept my thighs parted, forming the *V* that now framed Jacob's face, which was moving closer to me by the second. He licked his lips hungrily, and I shuddered at the sight of his tongue. I was ready and desperate for what he was about to do.

From the moment we'd started making out in the living room, juices had been flowing nonstop from my cunt. I could have gone on kissing him for much longer, but when he broke our embrace and suggested relocating to the bed, there was no way in hell I was going to say no. I knew what his suggestion meant: I'd soon be feeling his lips and tongue against my aching sex.

Jacob had undressed me quickly, and although I'd reached for his fly—wanting to grab hold of his big, hard cock—he'd stopped me before I could lower his zipper, telling me we'd have time for that later. I mollified myself by massaging the bulge in his jeans and stroking the ramrod-stiff outline of his shaft while imagining his cock sliding into me. His hands remained busy, too. With nimble fingers, he unbuttoned my blouse with one hand and unsnapped my bra with the other, all while we continued kissing. When my chest was bare, he lowered his head to my tits to lap circles around each hardened nipple and bite lightly at the tips.

My back arched from his mouth's ministrations, my breasts pressing against his face. Meanwhile, his hand traveled down to open my pants. I writhed against him, desperate for more direct contact. I would have been okay with only his hands at that point. Feeling his fingers against my slippery slit would have been enough to satisfy me, and I almost begged him to stroke me. However, I abstained, knowing that his mouth would feel even better.

Jacob tugged my jeans and panties over my hips, and I raised my ass to help him remove them. He lifted his head from my tits as he worked to pull the skinny ankles of my pants over my feet, but the thought of losing contact with his lips was unbearable. I pressed his face back to my bosom and wriggled the rest of the way out of my jeans myself. That left him free to resume tonguing my nipples, giving me a preview of what he would soon be doing to my even more sensitive clit, which was already throbbing.

Those pulsations only grew stronger when Jacob abandoned my breasts and began kissing and licking his way down my body. I expected him to stop at my sex, but he kept going. Painting his tongue over my inner thighs and brushing his lips along my calves, he made his way to my feet.

My breath quickened as he dragged his tongue along each arch. My boyfriend's mouth is magical; acts that would typically elicit fits of giggles actually get me aroused. The moment he sensed my complacency, he switched gears and sucked on my toes. Finally, he kissed the pad on the bottom of each foot before beginning his journey northward.

Jacob's lips brushed against my legs, his butterfly kisses leaving a trail of goose bumps in their wake. My heart beat faster in anticipation—and my cunt got even wetter. When he reached the juncture of my legs, he planted a kiss directly on my pulsating bull's-eye. My body heaved upward, and I cried out loudly. My unexpected reaction prompted him to ask if I was okay. "More than okay," I murmured, even more aroused than before.

I knew things were about to get wild, so I reached down and threaded my fingers through his hair to prepare myself for the onslaught. I was ready for him to really dig in, but he kept taking things slowly. He placed the same light, gentle kisses on my pussy that he'd used while making his way back up my legs. His lips worked over my outer labia and then slowly moved inward to the delicate petals, barely skimming over my heated flesh.

Sighing loudly, I opened my legs wider and gripped Jacob's head more tightly, tempted to press his handsome face against me and hold him there in my desperation for greater pressure. At the same time, I appreciated his deliberate efforts because I knew he was drawing out my pleasure, and in the end I would come much harder. But when he didn't instantly yield to my urgent hints, I backed off and let him do his thing, trusting that I was in capable hands.

Jacob continued teasing me, grazing my slick pink skin until his lips were glossy with my juices. Though he exhaustively covered almost the entire region, aside from his initial kiss, he'd managed to avoid one crucial spot—my throbbing clitoris. Regardless, there wasn't a part of my body that wasn't quivering, and my muscles clenched tight as I felt the rumblings of an orgasm building inside me.

Then Jacob switched from kissing to licking, and my breath grew shallow. He swiped his tongue along my entire slit, and in the process, made contact with my swollen clit. His glancing touch was not enough to make me come, but it definitely stoked the flames of my desire. Continuing his teasing, he flicked lightly at my petals and upped the ante by slipping a finger into my hole.

First, he penetrated me with only the tip and played around the edges of my opening. Then the rest of his digit followed. When he was buried to his bottom knuckle, he caressed me from the inside before starting to plunge in and out with a measured rhythm. All the while, he continued licking and sucking my slippery folds, and the double assault was so relentless that my eyes shut tight and my head whipped back and forth on the pillow.

Though my body was demanding satisfaction, I wasn't ready to come yet, and mustering all the willpower I possessed, I somehow managed to stave off the impending orgasm. The thrusts of his finger became more forceful as he moved his tongue in ever-narrowing circles around my button, which was now so hard it ached. I bore down against the mattress and tightened my grasp on Jacob to prepare myself.

My boyfriend flicked at my clit with the tip of his tongue, transforming the quaking in my belly into a series of small spasms. His finger continued thrusting into me, and I was certain he could feel the pulsations of my flesh. That felt delightful, but it was nothing compared to when he wrapped his lips around my clit and sucked hard. I was instantly consumed by a wave of body-shaking pleasure.

As my climax overwhelmed me, my thighs snapped shut against his head. However, my tenacious lover did not let my actions impede his. He used two fingers of one hand to spread my nether lips while the index finger of the other remained buried inside me. Although his movements were now more limited, he persisted in buzz-sawing my clitoris, making me come again, and my fingers dug into his scalp as I announced my release.

Just when I thought things couldn't get any better, Jacob wrested a hand from between my thighs, positioned it at one breast and strummed the nipple until I cried out. My body quivered wildly, and thanks to his ceaseless efforts I was soon approaching yet another peak. Then his fingers closed tight against my nipple, giving it a sharp pinch that sent me into the stratosphere.

With this climax, my ass rose off the mattress so high that my cunt mashed against my partner's mouth. He anticipated my motion and moved with me, not missing a beat as he kept licking and sucking me.

My boyfriend's mouth took me to another level. My moans turned to wails and then a series of gasps as my clit became hypersensitive. I tried begging him to stop, but he kept going, and I quickly realized that he couldn't really understand my hoarse pleas because my thighs were still clamped against his ears. I opened my legs and, somewhat reluctantly, urged his face away from my spasming pussy.

Thus released, Jacob sat up and looked at me, his cheeks flushed. I pulled him toward me, and as we embraced, he slipped his tongue into my mouth. I sucked at it, delighting in the flavor of my salty-sweet nectar as we rolled around on the mattress, and I soon found myself stretched out on top of him, his stiff cock pressed against my stomach.

I'd thought I'd have—and need—a moment to catch my breath, but I quickly decided that wasn't necessary. Instead, I wanted to return Jacob's favor. I knew he'd appreciate that because I felt his throbbing dick nudging my belly. I moved again, but this time he reached down, grasped my asscheeks and tried to pull me up to mount him. A postorgasm fuck was a tempting proposition, but I had other plans.

I gave Jacob one last tongue-filled kiss, before breaking away to buss his cheek and then suck his earlobe, something that always drives him nuts. This time was no exception, and he writhed beneath me and groaned with pleasure as I switched to the other lobe. The next time I looked at his face, his eyes were shut, but he was grinning from ear to recently sucked ear, so I knew it was time to start moving lower.

I spent a moment sucking at his neck, stopping short of leaving a mark, and then I trailed my lips along his collarbone and down to his broad chest. Jacob's nipples are as sensitive as mine, possibly even more, so I spent a few minutes at each, flicking my tongue over the tips and biting down gently. This elicited another series of groans, and when I reached down to grasp his manhood, I noted that his shaft was even harder than before.

I stroked him a few times, and his chest rose and fell as he took a series of deep breaths. If I wasn't careful, his load was going to end up all over his stomach. I wanted that tasty treat in my mouth, so I let go of his shaft to trail kisses down his stomach, much like he'd done to me earlier. However, unlike him, when I reached his pelvis I stopped there—I didn't have the patience for a trip to his toes and then back up—but I did decide to tease him a little first.

Reaching Jacob's cock, I ignored his shaft and crown and headed right for his balls. I heard his breath catch as I skimmed my lips over them. When I placed a kiss on each, his body tensed, so I started sucking on his sac.

I sucked hard at one firm orb, shifting it back and forth with my tongue. Then, when my boyfriend started groaning loudly, I switched sides and engulfed the other one. He responding by grabbing my shoulders as though I were the only thing keeping him tethered to earth. His body undulated wildly as I continued mouthing the soft skin of his sac.

When it was time to shift gears, I released his balls and wrapped my fingers around the base of his shaft. Holding him still with a tight fist, I kissed up one side of his length and then back down the other, applying just enough pressure to titillate him without exciting him too much. Also, with each trip up and back, I avoided contact with his cockhead. And doing that was no small feat because I was dying to give in to my urges and lick his dick like an ice-cream cone.

Taking long, slow laps, I took particular pleasure in teasing him, until Jacob gasped, "Please suck me!"

Looking up at him through my eyelashes, I gave him a big smile and then moved so my mouth hovered directly above his crown. Then I swooped down as if to swallow him whole, but at the last minute kissed only the very tip. Jacob gave an anguished cry as I licked pre-ejaculate off his head. He seemed to have forgotten that he'd put me through the same "torture" a mere half hour earlier. Still, he sounded so pitiful that I swooped down once again, this time engulfing his entire head with my welcoming mouth.

My lips smacked as I sucked him hungrily, feeling his knob

swell even larger against my tongue. Precome leaked from the tip so I licked up as much of the briny fluid as I could, and then I slowly started moving lower, sliding my mouth down his length. I could feel his shaft throbbing in a steady rhythm as I swallowed it inch by inch, and the pace of the pulsations increased as he grew more aroused. As soon as my chin came to rest on his sac, I began humming a little tune.

Jacob moaned at the vibrations now racing through his body. Still humming, I reascended, letting him feel the pressure of my tongue on the underside of his shaft as I dragged my lips over it. When I once again reached the summit, I suckled the tip until more of his fluids leaked onto my tongue, and then I took another trip down his shaft, aiming for the very bottom.

When my nose brushed his pubic curls, he let go of my shoulders and grabbed my head to guide me. He started at a leisurely pace, and I rose and fell rhythmically on his unflagging erection, my long brown hair brushing his stomach each time he was completely buried in my throat. To assist him, I kept my lips locked securely around him and swished my tongue back and forth over the bottom of his prick, which grew even thicker as a result of my efforts. Then, when I applied more pressure, he began guiding my head at a swifter pace, which alerted me that his climax was approaching. To help him reach his limits, I began moving the fist that had been holding him steady, stroking him at the same pace as my lips were sucking him.

That's when he grabbed the sheet beneath him, much like I had done earlier. The sounds he made became guttural and animalistic; I quickened my pace, tightened my fist and swallowed hard, so that my throat muscles once again constricted around his shaft. Then I started humming again, this time more loudly to let him really feel the impact of my vocal chords. I reached up and squeezed his balls to trigger his release.

The effect was immediate. Jacob grunted, and then his cock throbbed one, two, three times before he began to shoot his load. The first volley contained a considerable amount, but I kept sucking him, eliciting another salvo from deep in his balls. He tasted delicious, and each burst of his warm cream inspired me to work his dick more intensely. I jerked his shaft rhythmically and swallowed until I was certain he was totally empty.

Jacob pulled me off him as I swallowed the last few drops of his load. Moving so that we were face-to-face, I kissed him with sticky lips, and I could feel his mouth move into a smile. I was smiling, too, still basking in the afterglow from bringing my boyfriend to an explosive orgasm as well as from my own recent thrilling climax.

Lying there in each other's arms, we were about to fall asleep before we realized that it was only seven thirty. So we got up, went back to the living room and resumed watching the movie that had gotten us into bed in the first place. Before long, it was time for round two!

Screaming Orgasm

CHLOE PARKER

When I first started as a cocktail waitress at the hot new club downtown, I had a difficult time telling the different drinks apart. Which was the Slippery Nipple and which the Cupid's Kiss? Which was the Ménage à Trois and which a Screaming Orgasm? My bartender boyfriend, who had gotten me the job, offered to help.

"I'll give you a little after-hours coaching, Chloe," said Ryan. "Let's take a mini-vacation this weekend, and we'll get in some practice."

That sounded good to me. I let Ryan choose the spot, and soon we were settling in at a beachside hotel not far from our Santa Barbara home. While he unpacked, I raided the minibar, lining up the liquors and waiting for him to give me the rundown. But apparently Ryan had other ideas. When he walked into the living room of the suite, he chuckled at the colorful arrangement of tiny bottles on the kidney-shaped glass coffee table.

"I thought I was going to be your willing pupil all weekend," I said.

"You are, cutie. You are." He ran his hands through my long blonde curls with an amused look on his face.

"Then why are you laughing?"

"Have a little faith, Chloe," Ryan said, smiling at me, his blue eyes glittering with lust. "We're going to get started right away. And your first lesson is about Sex on the Beach."

I knew that drink was concocted with several ingredients, including vodka and peach schnapps. But it seemed that Ryan had his own recipe. He picked me up in his muscular arms and carried me over his shoulder down the hallway to our Hawaiian-themed bedroom. A metallic photomural of a Maui sunset gleamed on one wall, and the bedspread was covered with tiny palm trees and pink flamingos. Ryan tossed me right onto the center of the mattress and started to lift up my flirty white sundress.

"Wait," I admonished him, modestly adjusting my hem to cover my naked thighs. "I thought we were going to study drinks."

"I'm going to teach you about sex on the beach," he corrected me. "It looks like you're on a beach now, right?"

I looked around us, taking in the tropical decor—from the wallpaper to the lampshades with tiny shells hot-glued to their fringes. "Right," I nodded.

"So close your eyes and enjoy."

"Ryan—" I said in mock protest, feeling his fingers already

inching up my tanned thighs to reach for the waistband of my panties. "But you promised to be my teacher."

"Oh yeah, baby," he answered as he tossed my white satin panties across the room and then began to untie the laces of my white espadrilles. "I'll teach you things you never even thought of." Even *I* had to laugh at that.

After undoing the bow at the top of my dress, Ryan pulled that off me as well. Entirely nude, I was spread out like a decadent dessert on the bed. Then he climbed between my legs and settled down comfortably. Before I could think of anything else to say about our discarded lesson plans, he sealed his warm mouth to my pussy, his tongue flicking between my nether lips to sweetly stroke my clit in a little welcoming motion. As Ryan ate me, I lost all sense of myself. The sensations became so overpowering that I couldn't speak, think or hardly even breathe.

Ryan knows how to please me. He starts off strong, then retreats, teasing and taunting, making me wait before coming at me once again with full force. By the time he's ready to fuck me, I've experienced several earth-shattering orgasms and my pussy is dripping with sex juices. I had a feeling this afternoon would be no different.

Thoughts of memorizing all sorts of drinks quickly faded from my head, and I sucked in my breath as he started to trace indecent designs up and over my clit. My body responded automatically, my own creamy nectar flooding his tongue. I was dripping-wet in seconds, and my erotic scent seemed to fill the room. Could Ryan tell how turned on he'd made me in mere minutes? I was certain that he knew when he said, "Look at you. You're already so slick and wet for me. We should name a new drink after you. A Slippery Chloe."

I giggled while his tongue continued to tickle me in the most intricately delicious manner, making my whole body tremble with unabashed pleasure. At first, I worked to hold myself totally still, basking in his attention. But as he continued to tease me, I couldn't control myself. I grabbed onto his soft, dark hair with both hands, forcefully pressing his mouth harder against my pussy. I wanted him to continue for hours, or days, until I lost track of how many climaxes I'd experienced. However, despite my impatience, Ryan worked slowly, behaving very differently than when he is behind the bar, where he is all speed and sparkle. He was certainly taking his time, paying careful attention to all of my desires. He used his knowledgeable hands to spread my plump pussy lips wide apart. He kissed and licked me so sweetly, using his lips to ring my clit, sucking me until my undulating hips started to beat a sexual rhythm against the bed. As heavenly as it all was, I suddenly wanted more.

"Please," I finally said, "I need you."

"You have me, Chloe." His words were muffled against my wet flesh, and the thrilling vibrations worked through my pulsing pussy so that for a moment I couldn't even repeat my request. If he kept talking to me like that, with his mouth pressed tightly against me, I would come from that sensation alone. But after taking a moment to recover, I told him what I wanted. For some reason, I didn't think he would mind.

"I need to taste you," I explained. My voice sounded raw, husky with want.

"That's for later, baby," he said with a wicked grin, his lips glossy from my juices, a look that turned me on even more. "You're trying to skip ahead in your lessons—from amateur to expert."

"I'm no amateur when it comes to sucking your cock," I said, pulling hard on his hair so that he'd look up at me again. Staring deep into my eyes, he gave me a sly grin. Not wasting another second, he stripped out of his jeans and T-shirt. I admired his hard, corded muscles, flat belly and strong chest as he approached the bed, his erect cock leading the way. He climbed back onto the mattress and slid his six-foot-two body around so that his hips were positioned over my head and his stiff member butted against my mouth. My heart beat extra quickly when I saw how ready he was; I was ready, too. I wrapped my hand around his girth and brought his cockhead to my lips. Then I opened my mouth and drew him inside.

Ryan's cock slid back and forth between my lips. I started to gently suck on him, then I drew the entire length of his shaft down my throat, swallowing all of him. Ryan groaned and lifted his hips, helping me by plunging even deeper down, then slowly withdrawing. Each time he moved, he thrust toward my parted lips while his tongue flicked out and swiped at my clit, so that together we made one big circle of pleasure, linked and unbreakable.

For a moment, I was so taken with sucking his cock that I hardly paid attention to the way he was touching me between my legs. But then the warmth of his tongue started to ignite me again, and I felt a smoldering climax building up within me. I came quickly with Ryan's cock pulsing in my throat, and I moaned at the power of my orgasm. And when my blissful cries vibrated along his shaft, Ryan started to come, thrusting even harder before shooting his load down my throat. I swallowed every drop.

"So that's my favorite version of sex on the beach," Ryan said with a smile as he moved his body up on the bed to cradle me in his arms. "Although different bartenders may have other techniques," he added.

I nodded, trying to imagine me and Ryan enjoying some "sex on the beach" at work. I pictured him placing me on the highly polished counter of the bar and eating me in front of all our patrons before climbing up there himself and joining me in a sixty-nine. The thought gave me a little shiver, and I almost missed his next statement, which was: "So, are you ready for lesson number two?"

After a climax like that, I was more than happy to continue playing Ryan's game. He obviously had our syllabus all planned out. Ryan disappeared down the hall for a moment before returning with a hand mirror. I had no idea what this was for, but Ryan began to explain. "We're going to move right on to a Pink Lady," he said, his face still flushed from his recent climax.

"What exactly do you mean?" I asked, amused.

"I want you to see exactly how pretty and pink you are between your legs," Ryan continued. I felt myself blush as dark as a maraschino cherry as he handed the mirror to me. "Now, spread your pussy lips, Chloe. I want you to look at yourself."

My blush intensified. I felt as if the hot summertime sun really was beating down on me. I hadn't ever done anything like that before. Yes, I had a vague idea of what my pussy looked like, but I'd never observed it up close and personal. And certainly never with an audience!

Under Ryan's steady guidance, I used one hand to part my lips, the other to hold the mirror so I could see between them. This wasn't an easy task. Ryan had gotten me so wet that my pussy lips were still slick with my nectar. Each time I tried to spread myself apart, my fingers slipped in my juices. Finally, Ryan took the mirror from me and angled it just so, leaving both of my hands free to explore. Nobody had ever asked me to touch myself while he watched, but Ryan was so sexy and insistent that I was getting turned on by being exposed to his unrelenting gaze.

"Now, touch your clit gently. Really gently. Lightly tap it." I was still reeling from my first orgasm, and I found that I almost came again just from the faintest flicker of my fingertips on my clit. He must have known that would happen because he said, "Softer, baby. Softer. I don't want you to come again just yet."

I did my best to obey. I stroked my clit with the lightest, feathery motion I could possibly manage. As I did, Ryan asked, "See what a pretty pink lady you are? Now, show me how you like to touch yourself."

"How I like to touch myself?" I stared at him, still blushing.

"You know, when you're by yourself."

Stroking my aroused pussy was easier to do in front of Ryan while he was giving me explicit instructions, but the whole episode suddenly seemed much more personal and revealing once he stopped giving me orders. I was secretly emboldened by the sexy feeling growing inside me. With my shyness fading fast, I started to slowly finger myself. I didn't touch my clit directly, but I made graceful looping circles around it. Ryan watched for several minutes, and then as I got more and more aroused, he got even closer to me, nestling right up between my thighs, his breath caressing me along with my fingers. In moments, he'd taken over for me. This was an entirely different experience from the way he'd eaten me only minutes before. He seemed to have instantly memorized my favored rhythm, using the tip of his tongue like a perfectly spiraling finger.

"Oh god," I sighed, falling back against the pillows and letting my hands slip away.

"No, baby. You don't get to relax. You have to work, too."

I peered up at him curiously. "I have to work?"

"Yes, help me. Hold yourself open."

It was an effort to do what he asked, but I obeyed. I spread my lips wide apart for him as Ryan began to make diamond patterns around my clit, not touching me directly, but skating his tongue up and around that hot little button. I couldn't believe that I was going to come again so quickly, but I was. I let out a helpless squeal of warning and then I came, hard and fast, with my spasming pussy pressed tightly to Ryan's face, once again coating him with my creamy juices. My climax went on and on, shaking my entire body, making me tremble and rocking the bed. Ryan pushed back from me and licked his lips with an intense look on his face. I slid back down on the pillows again, completely demolished by the pleasure I'd just experienced.

"Don't get that look, baby," he said.

"What look?"

"That finished look," he continued. "We're far from done."

"Oh, Ryan," I sighed. My body was still shaking. What did he want from me? How much more could I take?

"We have one more lesson," he said, "at least, one more for the night." With that, he slid up my body, positioning himself with his cock nestled against my mouth. I parted my lips and took him in, getting ready to suck him off again, but Ryan had other ideas. As soon as the tip of his cock was wet, he moved back down my body and slid inside of my cunt. He thrust into me several times, and my body responded with tight contractions around his cock. Then, without warning, he pulled out again and slid back up on the bed. I bathed his cock with my tongue, relishing the taste of myself on his hard shaft. Then back he went, thrusting into me forcefully. I felt as though my body were melting into the mattress. I could hardly move, undone by pleasure as Ryan continued to take turns fucking my mouth and my pussy. My arousal soaring, I was soon tugging on him, letting him know when it was time to return to my mouth, desperate to taste myself again. I loved the flavor of my juices mingling with the first drops of his precome. I slid my tongue along the underside of his shaft as I sucked him hard. Ryan ran his fingers through my hair, but when he started to approach his peak, he pushed me away.

Back down my body he went, this time flipping me over so that he could take me from behind. He fucked me doggie-style for the last part of the ride, his hips bucking against mine, slamming into me forcefully. As he continued to fuck me, he slid one hand beneath my body to flick my clit. Between the fucking and the clit-strumming, I was soon coming powerfully, for the third time of the evening.

"Let it out, baby," Ryan crooned, and I found my voice, growing louder and louder as the contractions pulsed throughout my body. I was screaming before I realized it, and Ryan began shooting his hot load inside me. When he finally finished coming, he slipped out of my quivering pussy and then collapsed against my body so that we were both wet and sticky, sealed together with our abundance of juices.

"Oh god," I sighed contentedly. "That was amazing."

"No," Ryan said, grinning at me. "That's what I call a Screaming Orgasm."

I laughed out loud, realizing that I still didn't know any more about which drink was which. But I will certainly admit this: I was looking forward to more of Ryan's after-hours instruction.

Secret Appetites

Adam Vane

My girlfriend, Rita, has always been the quiet type. An artist, she expresses herself with colors and brushstrokes rather than words. But if she ever gave up her artistic endeavors, she'd make the perfect librarian. In fact, her quiet nature is what first drew me to her. We met at a crowded party, where boisterous, sociable people were creating a considerable racket. Cool, calm and collected, Rita stood out from the others. I took in her good looks, that shy doe-eyed gaze, and hurried over to introduce myself.

We hit it off instantly—I'm a DJ, and my outgoing personality complements her more reserved style. Yet when we're together, I have always been able to coax her out of her introspective shell—at least everywhere except in bed. That's because during sex, she gets even quieter. Her body shakes with silent tremors, but her lips remain closed.

I don't need her to scream or howl or shriek to let me know when she's excited. Her cheeks flush, blooming rosy pink against her pale skin. Her fingers dig into my shoulders, and she raises her hips upward as I thrust forward. And then of course, there's her pussy. All I have to do is test, with my fingers, tongue or cock dipping inside her, to know she's wildly excited. But other than that, I have to guess what she wants and when she's ready to switch positions or try something new.

I decided that I'd had enough. I was going to make her tell me exactly what she wanted in bed, no matter how much she blushed. I especially wanted her to tell me how she liked to have her pussy eaten.

"What do you like?" I murmured over coffee at our favorite outdoor café.

"What do I—"

"Like," I repeated.

She looked up at the handwritten chalk menu on the posted blackboard. But I quickly continued. "Not for breakfast. In bed. Are you satisfied with what we do together? Are there things you wish I'd do more often?"

Her pale cheeks glowed an instant crimson. "You know what I like, Adam—"

"I don't know," I countered. "That's why I want you to tell me."

She shook her head, her long chestnut-hued hair falling in front of her face, momentarily hiding her flush, although I knew full well it was still there.

"You're not really that shy," I said teasingly. "Remember, I've seen you. I know what you look like when you come. The way your eyes glow. The way your mouth opens so hungrily. And I know there's a part of you that's dying to tell me. Or, better yet, to show me."

She put up a hand, trying to stop the conversation.

"Not here," she said.

"Then where?"

"At home—"

I put money down on the table for our espressos. "Great. Let's go."

"Now?" she asked, shocked.

"Do you have other plans? More pressing plans than spending the day teaching me how to make you come with the tip of my tongue on your throbbing little—"

"Stop!" she demanded, giggling, pulling me through the wrought-iron gate and onto the street. "I'll tell you. I promise," she insisted. "Just wait until we're home."

"Why should I stop?" I taunted her. "Am I making you wet?"

"Yes." The heels of her black leather boots *click-clacked* on the sidewalk, and I thought I caught a different air about her, an air of authority, as if she'd decided to take charge of the situation. I liked this new attitude, and I fell easily into step beside her.

"I am?" I pressed onward, delighted. "You're telling me that you're wet right now? Inside those tight jeans, your creamy juices are—"

"Flowing," she finished for me. "When you talk dirty, you turn me on."

"What else do I do that turns you on?"

Her cheeks flaming a bright pink, she continued, clearly feeling freer now that we were climbing the front stairs to our apartment. "When you go down on me."

"Ah," I smiled at her boldness. "You like that, do you?"

"Mm-hmm." Her key turned in the lock, and then she pulled me into our living room and pushed me down on the gold velvet sofa.

"What do you like about it?"

Surprisingly, she didn't hesitate a moment. It was as if she'd considered this question before and had an answer at the ready, like pageant contestants when they reveal how they'd like to change the world. "The way your tongue makes those amazing circles around my clit," she said dreamily, "especially when you start before I can take my panties off. As if you can't wait for me to be completely undressed."

"I can't wait," I explained. "Sometimes you look too good."

"And then," she continued, "when you get me right on the edge with your mouth against my panties, that's almost unreal. It makes me wish I could beg you to tear my panties off me."

"So why don't you beg me?"

She shrugged. "I thought you wanted to be in control."

"If you're begging me for something, then I *am* in control."

She grinned broadly. "I never thought of it that way."

While she was talking, she was stripping. By the time she'd finished, her pale-blue cardigan and tight white T-shirt were draped over the back of the wicker rocking chair and her jeans lay in a puddle on the hardwood floor. She was down to a lilac camisole and a pair of matching panties. Man, did she look good, a long-limbed goddess with shoulder-length brown hair, bright-blue eyes and plump, pouty lips.

She let me admire her lanky figure—perky breasts, slim waist and hips I love to hold onto—before settling herself on the sofa at my side, spreading her long legs and looking over at me appraisingly.

"So, Adam," she said, in a powerfully sexy voice I hardly

recognized as coming from my formerly reserved girlfriend. "What are you waiting for?" And even though my quiet little vixen had never uttered a single command before, I snapped to it as if she were a drill sergeant. I pulled her forward so that she was lying flat on her back with a pillow under her head, and then I bent to press my lips to her panty-clad pussy. I breathed in deeply and smelled her delicious scent, and I knew then that she'd been telling me the truth: My words had turned her on. There was no doubt about it. She was all revved up and ready to go.

"Wait, Adam!" she insisted before my tongue could make even the first round of concentric circles. "Don't start at the finish line. Work your way up from the bottom." As soon as she spoke, she covered her mouth with the back of her hand, as if shocked by her own intensity. "Was that too bossy?"

I shook my head, smiling at her. It was precisely what I'd been fantasizing about for so long. "You tell me whatever's in your head. I want to hear it all. Describe each step for me the way you see it in your mind. Do you think you can do that?" She nodded. "So start."

"Kiss me slowly," she said, her voice wavering.

At her words, I began to kiss my way up her legs, starting at her petal-pink painted toes and then moving back and forth from one long, slender leg to the other.

"Now, touch me," she continued, her tone growing stronger. "Use the tips of your fingers so that you're almost tickling me, but not quite."

At her instruction, I massaged her butter-soft skin with my fingertips while I moved higher and higher with my kisses. When I finally reached the cleft between her legs, she was squirming on the sofa, her hips beating a soft tattoo against the golden pillows. I could see how aroused she was by the damp spot growing at the center of her panties. I pressed my lips against her through the shimmering silky material, and Rita groaned and raised her hips clear up off the sofa.

"That's right, Adam," she cooed, her inhibitions about being too bossy evaporating by the second. "Now, make circles with your tongue right around my clit."

I tricked my tongue in dainty circles all over her pussy, avoiding her pearl, but coming as close as I possibly could. I used my tongue and chin, and even my breath to warm her up. As I traced closer and closer, I felt her entire body trembling, and her reaction let me know that I was doing something right.

"Come closer." Her voice was suddenly hoarse with unabashed lust. "Closer and closer to my clit with each spiral of your tongue."

My cock throbbed fiercely in my khakis. This is what I'd asked for, and she was more than delivering, giving me a play-by-play of exactly what she wanted me to do. I'd never experienced anything sexier in my life.

"Oh god," she sighed, "don't stop. Please don't stop."

I obeyed her desire, ringing her clit more firmly, as if it were a bull's-eye that I was directly homing in on. When I reached the center, Rita moaned loudly with delight. I could hardly believe my ears. I'd never heard her do anything loudly in all of our time together. I was thrilled, but I kept my cool. Gently, I continued to lick her clit through her panties, but I also used my tongue to press forcefully against her, giving her the pressure I knew she craved. Again and again, I stroked her clit with the flat of my tongue, and I felt her squirming and wriggling beneath my careful ministrations. Finally, she could stand it no longer and used her own fingers to pull her panties to the side, revealing her hairless pussy.

"Don't just look at it," she demanded. "Lick it. Kiss it. Suck it." This time there was no blush to follow her command, no hesitation or worry that she was offending me by taking charge. I got the feeling that she was growing completely comfortable with telling me what to do. And she didn't have to tell me twice. I used my hands on her inner thighs to part her legs even wider, and then I resumed my previous actions, only now when my tongue met her bare-naked skin, I could taste her exquisite honey and feel for myself exactly how dripping wet she was. When I gazed up at her face, I saw that her eyes were shut tight and her full lips were parted. She seemed to be whispering something, but at that point it was hard to distinguish instructions from random words of pleasure that she could no longer contain.

"Like this?" I prompted, my words decadently muffled by her sweet pussy.

"Oh yes," she moaned, her hands finding the back of my head and pushing me even more firmly against her. I licked and lapped at the flood of juices that rushed to meet my tongue, and then I made a circle with my lips and sucked hard on her clit. Her cry of pleasure had my heart throbbing. I had never heard such joyful noises from her before. They made me happy, sure—but more than that, they made me desperate to fuck her.

My mission intensified as I worked harder to bring her to climax. I had it in mind to bend her over the sofa as soon as I felt her orgasm pulse through her body. Rita, however, had other plans for us. She twined her fingers in my thick dark hair and pulled me back when she was on the edge. I felt her slippery juices coating my lips and chin, but Rita had no qualms about pulling me up her body so that she could kiss me.

Then she grasped one of my hands and brought it to her mouth. Slowly, she licked and then sucked on my fingers. In seconds, I realized that she was still telling me what to do, though now she was using actions rather than words to convey her desires. I quickly dove back between her legs and mimicked the motions of her mouth on my fingertips, using the same spirals and the same pressure against her budding clit. As her arousal built, so did the manner in which she orally teased my fingers. She sucked harder, and I sucked harder. She moaned, and I moaned, and then her whole body began to shake. I knew that the sound of my voice reverberating through her had brought her a wave of pleasure she was not expecting. For a moment, her instructions stopped. She didn't seem to know how to continue, but I sensed what she needed and I took over. Yet Rita would have none of that. She gripped my hair again and pulled tight. I looked up at her face, surprised at the commanding expression I found there.

"I'm not done," I insisted, licking my top lip to catch a wayward drip of her delicious juice.

"I know you're not."

"Then what?"

"You said you wanted me to tell you what I wanted." I nodded in response. "Well, I want to suck you off while you make me come."

As soon as she said the words, I discovered that I wanted that, too. I stripped out of my clothes, then climbed astride her, head to toe. Her mouth was open and ready, and I pumped the head of my cock between her parted lips, feeling that delicious warm wetness envelop me. I started thrusting forward, but Rita slapped me firmly on the ass to stop me. I drew in a deep breath and held myself in check.

"I want to suck you," she said, pulling away from my cock. "You don't do the work. You let me do it."

I exhaled in a great rush, almost disbelieving that this woman telling me what was going to happen was my sweet girlfriend. Then I shut my eyes as she brought the head of my pulsing cock into her mouth and started to suck. My mouth fell open, and my whole body tensed— muscles locked, back tight. Rita worked me with finesse, employing her lips, her tongue, the very indents of her cheeks as she sucked me like a powerhouse. She treated me so intensely that I didn't realize I was being lax in my duties on her pussy until she paused.

"You're not done, Adam," she reminded me.

"Oh, yeah," I muttered, feeling slightly light-headed. "Oh, right." And I brought my head back down between her legs and started to lick her again. Her creamy juices were slippery on my tongue, and she was the most aroused she'd been all morning. But for once I didn't have to resort to reading the code of her body in order to tell what was going on. This time Rita gave me verbal cues, keeping up the game I'd started at the café. She pulled away from delivering that beautiful blow job long enough to tell me when she wanted me to suck harder, when to thrust my tongue inside her, when to overlap my fingers and fuck her pussy.

And finally, she told me when she was ready for my cock.

"Put it in my pussy," she insisted. "I need you inside me, Adam. Now!"

My cock was more than ready for her, and I was desperate to feel the welcoming embrace of her pussy tightening around it. I swiveled around on the sofa and felt her spread her pussy lips open with her fingers. Then with one thrust, I plunged inside. Instantly, I was rewarded with the delirious wetness that surrounded me. But even better than her clutching cunt were the sounds that Rita made, the moans that grew in volume as I continued to plunge into her hard and fast. I'd never heard her vocalize like that before, and her lustful noises turned me on more than anything I'd ever experienced.

"Keep going," I encouraged her breathlessly. "Don't you stop."

She didn't. Her voice grew louder and louder. We were connected so fiercely, so dramatically, that I felt we were actually one being—with one goal: to reach the end together. Rita was quiet for several minutes as we slid together, our bodies momentarily doing all the talking for us. But when I thrust in extra deep and pulled back out, Rita started to speak again.

"Faster," she purred. "Come on, Adam. I'm almost there. Please."

My heart sped up at her words, and I gave her exactly what she craved: faster, harder, more. And each time she told me what to do, I granted her request, because each of her demands mirrored my own desire as well. The desire to please her, to thrill her, to hear her scream when the pleasure broke within her and those walls came tumbling down.

"Don't stop talking," I gasped. "Come on, baby. Keep going. Keep telling me exactly what you're feeling."

When she climaxed, she made my dreams come true, my quiet girl turning into a screamer.

"Oh god, I'm coming. I'm coming, Adam!"—and I climaxed one second later, filling her up and then holding her so tightly she couldn't move. I thought of the first time we had sex and how much I loved being with her.

After our postorgasm embrace, I leaned back from her, looking down at her pretty face, and I was surprised to see a familiar blush coloring her cheeks. This time her blush wasn't one of after-climax bliss, but a sign of shocked self-consciousness. As I appraised her, she raised a hand to shield her face, but I would have none of that. We'd gone way past the hiding games she'd played for so long. I pulled her hand away and stared right at her.

"I can't believe it," she said shyly. "I've never done anything like that before."

"I loved every word you said," I assured her. "Every single noise you made in the heat of the moment. You have no idea how much you turned me on."

"Really, Adam?" she said, giggling, before quickly lifting her hand to her lips to cover her mouth. As she realized her habit of quieting herself, she pulled her hand away and instead brought her fingers to my mouth.

"From now on, I think I'll be doing a lot more with my mouth," she said, her voice suddenly much more commanding as she traced her delicate fingertips over my lips. My cock was already twitching in response to Rita's newfound confidence, and I couldn't get over this recently revealed side of my girlfriend and how hot she was making me for her.

When she slid her finger between my lips, wetting it on my tongue, she flashed me a wicked smile and said, "I think it's safe to say, your mouth will be doing a whole lot more for me, too." I could hardly imagine what other secret fantasies she had lingering beneath the surface, and I couldn't wait to find out.

Honky-Tonk Heat

Nancy Richman

There are two things I really love more than anything: good country music and going down on men. And since the kind of guys who turn me on are black-hatted country singers, I moved to Nashville as soon as I could.

I was twenty-three and single when I left my hometown and drove to Tennessee. After spending a night in Memphis, I made a pilgrimage to Graceland and then got back in my car and headed across the state to Nashville.

I'm a songwriter myself, and once I settled into a small apartment near the Cumberland River, I took some of my demo tapes and started making the rounds of the recording studios on Music Row. I also landed a part-time job tending bar in a honky-tonk in the Alley, as it's called—Printers Alley, where a lot of the best clubs in Nashville are located.

That's where I met Jesse. He was the lead singer in a band out of East Texas, and the first time I laid eyes on him, I immediately wanted his cock in my mouth. Lean and sinewy, with a mop of black hair and heavy-lidded brown eyes, he had exactly the kind of country outlaw look that does it to me. I loved his voice, too. A rich, lonely baritone. The way he slouched around the stage in his washed-out jeans and cowboy boots made my pussy dampen.

At closing time, Jesse was sitting at the bar, relaxing with a long-necked bottle of beer. Naturally, I spent as much time as I could hanging around him, and when he asked me for my phone number, I wrote it out in lipstick on a cocktail napkin.

"Well, thanks, darlin'," he said with a smile. "I'm going off to Galveston tomorrow, but I'll be back in town in a week. I'll give you a call then, okay?"

True to his word, Jesse called me a week later and asked me out for lunch. It was a little before noon and I was still in panties and a pajama top, with my hair up in curlers, but I was so anxious to see him that I told him to come right over. As soon as I got off the phone, I ran around frantically pulling myself together. I did my hair and makeup in record time, then put on a pair of skintight jeans and a tailored shirt with the tails tied beneath my breasts. I was giving myself one last look in the mirror when the doorbell rang.

"Hello there," Jesse said with a grin. "You're even sexier than I remembered."

"In this outfit? I just flung on any ole thing."

We ate at a barbecue shack right outside the city and then

went horseback riding along a sun-dappled trail in the foothills of the Smoky Mountains. And let me tell you, the sight of Jesse astride a big bay stallion really got to me. So did the constant friction of my pussy against the saddle, and the feel of my tits bouncing as we cantered along the trail.

After we returned our horses to the stable, we took a drive in Jesse's vintage Chevy and parked at a high lookout point that gave us a view for miles in every direction. It was getting on toward dusk, and the lower flanks of the mountains had turned purple with deep shadow. There were pools of fog gathering in the valleys, and the crowns of trees seemed to float in the mist like lily pads.

"That's Georgia over there," Jesse said, pointing to the southeast. "Pretty sight, isn't it?"

Presently we started making out—long, slow kisses that made me melt in both my heart and my panties. Before long Jesse's hand was on my breast, first through my shirt and then inside my bra, his finger rubbing my nipple. I returned the favor by cupping the crotch of his jeans and squeezing his growing bulge.

"Why don't you show me what you've got down there?" I murmured.

Unbuckling his silver-studded belt, he pulled down his fly and brought out his half-hard cock. My glance caused it to stir, and when I reached out and closed my fist around the shaft, I had a serious hard-on in my hand in about five seconds flat.

Fully erect, Jesse's cock was about average in length and nice and thick, with an unusually dark shaft, almost walnut in color. He was also uncircumcised and that excited me even more, as I love peeling back the foreskin and slowly revealing the naked glans.

When I did this to Jesse, I uncovered a dusky mauve knob already glistening with stickiness. I quickly bent over and consumed his entire cock, right down to the root.

"Damn!" he muttered in amazement. "Where'd you learn to do that?"

Instead of answering his question, I teased him by rising up off his length. Then I swallowed him again, inch by slow inch, until his pubic hair was tickling my lips. Pressing the underside of his shaft with my tongue and sucking forcefully enough to indent my cheeks, I slowly backed off once more and went to work on his crown. After swirling my tongue over and around the sensitive ridge, I ran his slippery glans back and forth across my lips just like I was putting on lipstick.

By this point, Jesse was dribbling so much precome that it was all over my mouth and hand and gleaming on his shaft. I was terribly hot myself, the taste and smell of his musk an irresistible aphrodisiac that aroused me immensely. Dizzy with lust, I tugged his jeans down past his hips and then snuggled into the warmth of his crotch and began licking his pendulous balls. I sucked and nibbled on the wrinkly skin of his scrotum for a while, and at last I opened wide and took as much of his sac into my mouth as I could.

That's one of my favorite moments in any blow job, and after gorging on his balls for a good long while, I licked my way back up his shaft and started slurping on the head. I guess I'd been working it for a good four or five minutes when Jesse began giving every indication that he was about to ejaculate. Groaning and squirming around, he kept trying to shove his cock back down my throat. To tease him a little more, I wrapped my fingers around the base of his shaft and tightened my grip, squeezing really hard to keep his semen from rising. Finally, I relented.

"Okay, now!" I cried. "Shoot your come!" As I relaxed my grip on his shaft, he arched his back and sent a geyser of semen into the air. Most of it landed on my lips, but by the time he spurted again, and then again, his dick was in my mouth and his hot cream was pouring down my throat.

Later that night, back at my place, we had another make-out session, first while still wearing clothes and then naked on my bed. I was more than happy to go down on Jesse again, but I'd barely begun to suck his cock when he pulled out of my mouth and gently pushed me against the pillows.

With a smile in his voice, he said, "You've been working too hard, little lady. Now just lie back and relax."

As he spread my legs with his hands, I closed my eyes and took hold of my breasts. I could feel his warm breath tickling my pussy, and then he started painting my labia with his tongue, sending shivers up my spine. Letting go of my tits, I reached down and opened myself with my fingertips. Then his mouth was on my opening and I moaned as I gave myself over to the pleasure that flooded my cunt and clit. When I brought my hands back to my breasts, I could smell the scent of my pussy on my fingers—the same rich perfume that Jesse was inhaling while his tongue went darting into my slit and then flashed across my clitoris.

"Yes, there!" I whimpered. "On my clit!"

Tenderly, belying his tough cowboy exterior, he drew my swollen nub between his pursed lips. A moment later, there was so much feeling in my throbbing clitoris that I had a dizzy illusion I was melting inside his mouth. The orgasm that followed was ravishing and deeply compelling, and for a few exquisite minutes, I disappeared and became part of him.

Given Jesse's occupation—he was on the road a good part of the year—I knew from the get-go that we wouldn't be having any sort of long-term monogamous relationship. Still, even though I wasn't seriously in love with him, I couldn't help missing him once he left Nashville and went out on an extended tour.

What happened next sure was a surprise, albeit a super-sexy one. Not long after Jesse left town, the phone rang. It turned out to be one of the women I worked with, Tina. Apologizing for bothering me at home, she explained why she was calling: She had played my demo tape for a young musician named Bill, and he was so impressed that he wanted to use one of my songs on his upcoming record.

Letting out a shriek of joy, I said, "You're kidding! Oh, that's great, Tina! I'm really thrilled!"

I was even more thrilled the following night, when she took me to a funky little roadhouse where Bill and his band were appearing. When she pointed him out onstage, I couldn't have been happier. Playing a beat-up acoustic guitar, he had the rangy, rawboned look of an Oklahoman cowboy, which is exactly what he was. He was definitely not a pretty boy. He had brownish hair bleached almost blond from the summer sun and a droopy Pancho Villa mustache. But to my eyes, at least, he was as sexy as springtime.

After the first set, Tina took me backstage and introduced me. Then at closing time, a whole crowd of us piled into several cars and went out on the town. In the course of things, Bill and I separated ourselves from the pack and spent a few hours in a bar, drinking beer and getting to know each other.

Toward sundown, I invited Bill back to my apartment for breakfast. When we got upstairs, I changed into shorts and a T-shirt and then went into the kitchen and brewed a pot of coffee. Bill sat at the table, chin in hand, quietly smoking a cigarette while I busied myself setting out plates and silverware. Moving back and forth between the table and the kitchen counter—whisking a few eggs in a bowl, dropping slices of bread into the toaster—I felt happy and lighthearted. I felt sexy, too, in my raggedy denim cutoffs and bare feet, my large breasts moving fluidly beneath my loose T-shirt.

Then the moment came when the sexual tension between us finally broke like a fever. As I leaned over the table to set down a cup in front of him, Bill put his hands on my hips and then casually, as if we were already lovers, reached beneath my shirt and palmed my heavy breasts. I blinked, opened my mouth to say something, flushed and finally settled into his lap and kissed him on the mouth.

While we were kissing, the toast popped up, but it didn't matter anymore—breakfast was long forgotten. I could feel Bill's penis stiffening beneath my ass while he fondled my breasts, and as my tongue darted into his mouth, my nipples and clitoris began to tingle. I was suddenly so hot for him that I could barely breathe. By the time we went into my bedroom, my panties were sticky and Bill was fully erect.

In a matter of moments, both of us were naked, and when I actually saw Bill's hard-on I thought I'd died and gone to heaven. His cock was long and extremely fat, with a massive and beautifully formed ruddy-colored glans.

He sat down on the edge of the bed, and I sank to my knees and placed his penis in my cleavage. Holding my breasts tightly together, I kneaded my soft flesh until a dribble of clear fluid emerged from the tip of his cock. As his stickiness smeared my skin, I let go of my tits and then bent over and took his hard-on in my mouth.

I couldn't deep-throat him, although I certainly tried; after repeatedly swallowing five or six inches I crouched lower and sucked on his balls. At the same time, I kept sliding my fist up and down the length of his slippery prick. When I heard him groaning helplessly, I released his cock, and then I stood up and palmed my breasts.

"Suck my tits," I whispered.

Not that he needed any encouragement: before I even had the words out, he squashed my breasts between his hands and applied his mouth to both nipples simultaneously. I always go crazy whenever anyone sucks on my nipples, and having Bill tongue them both at the same time made me nearly jump out of my skin.

"Ooh, nice, that's nice," I panted.

He kept sucking until a lovely warmth suffused my chest. The sensation in my nipples grew more intense, and little starbursts of feeling kept drifting from my tits down into my cunt. When I couldn't take it anymore, I pulled away from his mouth and pushed him back on the bed.

Climbing on top of Bill in a sixty-nine position, I presented my pussy to his face and wrapped my lips around his swollen cockhead. As I lowered my hips, he spread my buttocks with his hands and slipped his tongue into my dripping slit. His mustache tickled my lips, so I sat down more firmly and buried his face beneath my ass.

Almost immediately, the lingering sexiness in my chest flared up between my legs. It was a soft, delicate orgasm, tender and melting rather than sharp. For a brief moment, I took his cock out of my mouth and panted my way through my climax. Then, when the radiance in my belly began to fade, I opened wide and quickly swallowed most of his length.

I rarely come twice in a row, but soon I felt another orgasm stirring inside me. As it gathered force, I flexed my vaginal muscles and rubbed my labia across Bill's mouth until I had his tongue pressed against my button. *Don't move, don't move*, I thought, and then said it aloud.

He complied, and in the next instant the contractions were so strong that I cried out in bliss. I was still holding on to Bill's cock, but I wasn't really aware of it until it twitched in my fist. Just as his semen began gushing out, I stuffed him back into my mouth and swallowed his delicious seed.

A few weeks later, I was in the studio with Bill, listening to him record one of my songs. By that point, we'd had sex dozens of times, I suppose. More importantly, we'd fallen in love, so that each time Bill entered me, whether he was in my mouth or in my pussy, he entered even more deeply into my heart.

Tasting the Good Life

DAVID CARLSON

When I opened the invitation, the first image that came to mind was Vicki's curvaceous body filling out her sexy blue cocktail dress. The second image, which brought a smile to my face, was the vision of her down on her knees in that dress, sucking me off.

Formal affairs can be marvelously erotic. The room is usually full of short and low-cut dresses that expose expansive acreages of silky female skin. Then there are the long slinky numbers that flow gracefully over every luscious curve and give tantalizing glimpses of long, shapely legs. Also, I get to wear my tuxedo, which Vicki says really turns her on. It's not surprising at all then that these affairs arouse us and often entice us into some form of sexual activity.

Quite often this activity turns out to be wholly, or at least primarily, oral. Fired up by feasting all evening on the visual banquet, Vicki and I sometimes can't contain our sexual energy until we return home. We'll slip off to some hidden or secluded place and make love right there. And this erotic spontaneity is perfectly suited to the anywhere, anytime characteristics of oral sex.

The invitation we'd received was for a black-tie reception at the home of a local well-to-do arts patron. Vicki is on several committees, and we sometimes get invited to these sorts of affairs. I'm not too artistically inclined, but I certainly like the scenery. So I was looking forward to the evening.

The day started out normally enough, but it suddenly turned sour. Vicki's morning tennis match went three grueling sets before she lost to her archrival. Then on the way home, she ran out of gas and had to walk the remaining two blocks in a brief but torrential downpour. By the time she arrived, she was a soaked, dejected mess.

I helped her out of her clothes and into a hot shower before retrieving her car. When I returned she was lying facedown on the bed, a bath towel wrapped around her torso. Her head was half-buried in a pillow, her shoulder-length sandy-brown hair fanned out over it.

I sat on the bed and ran my hand lightly along her shoulders and neck. "Feeling better?"

"Uh-huh." Her voice was muffled by the pillow.

I started massaging her back, feeling the tension dissolve.

"This feel good?"

"Uh-huh."

I straddled her, pulled the towel aside and massaged away the remaining kinks. Just looking at her trim body was getting me hard. I leaned over to kiss the smooth skin of her shoulders, my tongue tracing lazy patterns as I worked my way up to her neck. Vicki melted completely and moaned her approval.

I spent a while on the side of her neck, then nibbled at her ear. "Do you want more?" I whispered.

"Uh-huh."

"Then turn over." As she did, our lips joined in a long, deep kiss that sent my pulse racing.

I set to work, using my mouth and tongue on her arms, her legs, her knees, the hollow of her ankles. Sometimes full, flat kisses. Sometimes gentle licks and pecks. And where I wasn't kissing I fondled with gentle fingers. In no time, Vicki was squirming on the bed and moaning.

I slid on top of her, crushing her body against mine. She lifted off my shirt, and our lips mashed together. I felt her breasts pressing against my chest. One of her hands worked its way down to my crotch, and she sensuously massaged my hard bulge. I was so turned on I was afraid that if she let my cock out, I might not be able to resist plunging into her. So I slid down, kissing her neck and chest. I stroked her tits before gently licking her nipples. She grabbed my head and arched her back as the tip of my tongue played over her little nubs.

Vicki's breasts are perfect handfuls, round and firm, with small nipples that stand quite erect at the slightest provocation. While I kissed one, I rolled the other between my fingers. Vicki gasped for air. I continued teasing her, kissing her flat stomach and rounded hips. I moved between her legs, delighting in her musky scent as I gently licked the tangy juice from her puffy outer lips. I drove my tongue into her pussy, probing and licking the soft, fleshy folds.

Vicki bucked her hips and roughly clutched at my hair. "Oh,

that's so good," was all she could say amid rhythmic moaning and panting.

I pressed my mouth to her sex as my tongue probed her hot tunnel. By the time I licked her swollen love button, she was close to climaxing. I flicked my tongue lightly over her clit, but also devoted attention to the sensitive area surrounding it. Meanwhile, my hands played over her breasts, ministering to her nipples with a light touch.

"You're driving me crazy!" she cried, her hips wriggling underneath me. "You've got me so hot." Her hands moved wildly between my head and her sides, clutching alternately at my hair and the rumpled bedsheet. "I think I'm going to explode."

After a few minutes at this plateau, I drove my tongue as far into her cunt as possible. I withdrew momentarily to suck on her clit before diving back in again. Vicki hurtled over the edge, squealing and gasping, her hips bucking wildly as an intense orgasm washed over her.

I kept my mouth pressed to her sex as her orgasm subsided, then crawled back on top of her. Taking her head in my hands, I gazed into her eyes. She looked like she had just run a marathon—and won. I kissed her forehead, her cheeks, her neck.

Vicki brought my face to hers, and we kissed deeply. They were long, gentle kisses at first, but soon our tongues got into the action, dancing around each other. Vicki's hips started writhing again, and her hands went to my pants. I rose up a little so she could undo them and push them down over my ass.

We were still enjoying juicy, wet kisses as she grabbed my stiff rod and brought it to the entrance of her pussy. I'm pretty beefy, but Vicki was so wet that I slid in effortlessly. And I was so stoked up from pleasing her that I immediately started pumping away, stroking into her with long, deep thrusts. Vicki's cunt muscles grabbed at me, and she pulled her legs up, rubbing her soft thighs along my sides and giving me a different angle of attack.

Burying my cock in Vicki's warm, wet tunnel, I pulled her up into a sitting position with her legs over my thighs. In this position, her tits were within easy reach of my mouth. I kissed and licked her nipples as she put her arms around my head and humped my cock.

Soon the room was filled with the sounds of grunting, groaning and panting. Vicki was going full speed again, slapping her thighs against mine. I moved my mouth from breast to breast, kissing and licking her womanly flesh, barely able to contain myself until she grabbed my head and held it to her chest. Her hips bucked as she came again. Then I let loose, thrusting into her furiously. I buried my cock in her pussy and my head in her tits as I pumped my load into her quivering tunnel. She held my head in place, muffling my growls in her flesh.

Our arms remained wrapped around each other, but we stopped moving. We were both coated with a sheen of sweat. Soon, my cock started to relax, but I was content to stay awhile in her welcoming warmth.

Eventually, Vicki looked at me and smiled. "Darn it. Now I'll have to take another shower." I couldn't help laughing at her.

Vicki and I relaxed for the rest of the day, enjoying each other's company, and by the time we started getting ready for the reception, we were already talking about sneaking away for an oral sex interlude.

"How do I look?" I asked, adjusting my bow tie.

Vicki came closer and straightened my tie. "Like a fox." Then she gave my crotch a squeeze. "Good enough to eat."

It was no surprise when, later that evening, Vicki started discreetly giving me "that look," the one that let me know she had trouble on her mind—the best kind of trouble. She was captivating in a short, elegant cocktail dress with spaghetti straps and a plunging neckline. Her eyes sparkled, and she shot me a naughty smile as she took two glasses of chardonnay from a server's tray.

I was engaged in conversation with a small group that included a curvaceous blonde whose bustier top afforded enticing views of her ample breasts. Vicki came up behind me, handing me a glass of wine. She pulled me slightly aside and, after discreetly flicking her tongue against my earlobe, whispered, "You look so hot. I want to suck that big cock of yours."

It sounded so delightfully nasty, especially the way she said it—with a soft, throaty voice bristling with sexuality. And my cock got the wake-up call. I abruptly excused myself, no longer interested in the conversation or in staring at Miss Cleavage.

She pulled me by the hand. "Feeling a bit feisty?"

I nodded and started looking for a convenient place, but Vicki had apparently already scoped out a secluded spot in the garden. It was perfect—a small gazebo, far enough away from the house and in the shadows of a laurel hedge. At night, you could see anyone approaching long before being seen. There was even a bench around the octagonal interior—a perfect place for a romantic tryst.

When we reached the gazebo, I pulled Vicki close to me. Our lips met, and for the first time that evening, I noticed her jasmine-scented perfume. She must have dabbed on a few extra drops before she'd suggested this rendezvous. As our tongues sought each other out, I cupped the back of her head.

I ran my hands down her neck and along her silky shoulders, then along her sides and over the curves of her hips. I reached the hem of her dress and instinctively started pulling up the garment, running my fingers along her nylons and across the smooth skin of her thighs. She was wearing thigh-high stockings for easy access. "I want to taste you," I whispered. But her hand was already going down to my fly, undoing it with practiced ease.

"Later," she said, kissing my cheek. "Right now I want your cock."

Who was I to argue? I stood before her as she perched on the edge of the bench. My dick was so hard that she had to undo my belt before she could pull my erection out. Vicki spread her legs so I could step between them, and her dress rode higher, exposing her thighs all the way up to the lacy tops of her stockings.

"Yum, yum, yum," she said, looking up at me with bedroom eyes. Even in the dim light I could see the reflection of her lust. "Good and hard, just the way I like it."

I was going to enjoy this, but so was she. Sometimes Vicki will play with me, teasing my cock with light kisses before taking me into her mouth. That night she got right down to business, wrapping her lips around the head, suckling it while she rolled her tongue over its surface. My eyes drifted between her long, sexy legs and her mouth working its magic on my manhood.

Her lips rode up and down my shaft, taking in a little more each time. I moaned, and my lids fluttered closed. But watching her is part of the fun, so I opened my eyes and carefully pushed Vicki's hair back from her face so I could clearly see my cock disappearing into her mouth. Every nerve ending in my body sparked each time her lips rode over the rim of my engorged head. Her loving mouth pumped me eagerly. The muscles in my groin tightened in response, and heat radiated through my entire being.

When she swallowed my entire length, I felt my cock pushing against the back of her throat. I groaned, and she withdrew slowly before giving my cockhead a few pecks as she caught her breath. "I love feeling your fat prick in my throat." Then she dove in and swallowed me once more.

I groaned again, casting a quick glance around us to make sure no one was within view—or earshot. My feeling of relief that we were still alone was quickly replaced by my rising lust. My knees became wobbly. I let go of Vicki's head and grasped the gazebo's railing for support as she swallowed my length again and again. "Oh, baby," I groaned. "I'm gonna burst!"

She withdrew only to say, "I'm counting on it." Then she kissed and licked up and down my shaft and my constricting scrotum before devouring me again, not as deeply, but at a faster pace. Perceptive lover that she is, Vicki knew when I was reaching my limit and ready to come. I felt the pressure build in my balls until it was uncontrollable. Her hands grabbed hold of my ass, and her lips surrounded me as I sucked in a deep breath and let go, spurting semen into her mouth.

Vicki held my sated member in her hand as my hardness slowly subsided. She licked off a final pearly drop of my load, then I made myself presentable once more. I pulled her up to me, and we kissed. Her tongue tasted of a mix of chardonnay and my come—a heady elixir. "I love how you suck me," I murmured against her lips.

"And I love doing it to you," she replied. She took my hand and guided it under her dress to her pussy. "See what it does to me?" She was soaking wet.

I was ready to drop to my knees right there, tux and all, but just then a group of people came out of the house and started ambling about in the garden. So we sat, side by side, on the bench. All they could see was a couple sitting in the gazebo, enjoying the evening air. What they couldn't see was that Vicki's dress was hiked up over her ass and I was slipping my finger in and out of her slick pussy.

By the time the people disappeared, Vicki was moaning softly.

"Your turn," I said. "But you need to keep watch."

"Mmm," was her only reply. I took that as a yes.

When Vicki leaned back against the gazebo wall, she could just see over the railing. Her dress was bunched, but otherwise we were safe. I squatted on my haunches and brought my mouth to her sex. Our position was a little awkward, but I sensed that I wouldn't be in this spot for very long. When Vicki is that excited, a few licks in the right place usually does the trick.

I lapped up her juices, attending to her swollen outer lips and relishing her taste. My hands found their way to her breasts, and I caressed them through her dress, feeling her hardened nipples. I rolled those tiny nubs between my fingers as I continued to tongue her clitoris.

That sexy combination set her to gasping. "Oh yeah, oh yeah," she moaned, over and over like a sensual mantra.

I ate her hungrily, fervently, and it wasn't long before she started flexing her thighs around my head and trying to stifle moans that came from deep within her. When she raised her hips off the seat and started convulsing, I went into maintenance mode, licking and kissing tenderly along the length of her sex. I kept my mouth against her twitching cunt until she let out a long breath of surrender.

When Vicki managed to speak again, it was with a deep, slow-motion voice. "Oh yeah."

We straightened ourselves up and returned to the party, slithering our way through the unaware throng. At the bar, one of Vicki's artist friends stood alongside us. "Great party, don't you think?" he queried.

"Excellent," I replied with conviction. Vicki and I quietly exchanged conspiratorial smiles. "Most excellent."

Pillow Lips

Fiona Hoffman

My husband is always eager to embark on a "lip service" adventure. He's an avid pussy man, constantly burying his face between my thighs. He also has the perfect cock for sucking. Matthew is thirty-three and very fit. His job as a massage therapist keeps him toned and lean. He's about six-foot-two-inches tall and 185 pounds and seductively good-looking, with a sweet baby-face, pillow lips and a roguish shock of black hair. He keeps his hair short on the sides but long on top, so a dark curl drifts across his forehead. Inside his underwear is the most delicious cock I've ever come across. It's thick and nearly eight inches long, with a wide plum-shaped head that feels like velvet against the back of my throat.

A fun game developed when Matthew and I had been married for three short months. We decided to call mutually designated evenings "lip service" night, meaning we could do whatever we wanted with our mouths.

We both enthusiastically enjoy oral sex, but sometimes we get swept up in the heat of newlywed passion and don't give it the appropriate attention. These special evenings give us the opportunity to indulge fully in one of our favorite erotic hobbies.

When we were dating, I would often get so ravenous for his cock that I would stop by his office to pay him a naughty visit. I loved engaging him at work when he was in between clients because it felt like we were getting away with something. One of these encounters occurred about a week before we got married, when I surprised him as he was finishing up some paperwork. I walked in, purposely clicking my heels on the hardwood floor. Matthew had his back to me and immediately stiffened when he heard my footsteps. He turned and flashed me a sexy grin.

He stood up, and I noticed a tent was already forming in his pants. His eyes traveled hungrily over my body. I am three years younger than Matthew and keep myself in shape with regular gym visits. My job as an interior decorator requires me to dress in office attire, and Matthew loves it when I'm in my work clothes. I like to tease as well as please my man, so that day I was wearing a short skirt with a matching jacket in "fuck-me fuchsia." Instead of panty hose, I always wear stockings and garters with patent-leather pumps to show off my toned legs. His appreciation clearly showed on his handsome face.

The pen he had been holding clattered to the floor. I strutted toward him and leaned in for a passionate kiss. He enveloped me in his arms, holding me against his muscular chest. I felt warmth begin to spread through my pussy, arousal dampening my panties as I took

Matthew by the hand and guided him to the bathroom in the back of his office.

Matthew grabbed a towel from a nearby shelf and draped it over the toilet seat to ensure that my clothes stayed pristine. Before sitting down, I slid my hands up under my skirt, pressing the delicate fabric of my panties deep into my cleft. When my undies were slick with my juices, I eased the garment down my thighs. Matthew's eyes drank in the sight of my exposed thighs and garters. I pressed my silky panties against his mouth and nose. His eyes closed as he breathed in my musk, and a low moan escaped his lips.

Matthew held my panties to his face to savor my fragrance as I tugged down his pants until they pooled at his ankles. I love the thrill and urgency of having sex half-clothed, so I left his shirt on. His boxers were easily lowered to his thighs, allowing his cock to spring free. I buried my face in his hot balls, inhaling his masculine scent. I lapped at them, swirling my tongue along their roundness. Matthew spread his legs for me, and a look of pure bliss washed over his clean-shaven face. I lightly sucked one ball at a time into my mouth, repeating the swirling pattern on each. His cock grew even harder, bobbing temptingly in front of my face.

I teased his balls and the base of his cock with my manicured fingernails. He stiffened and strained toward me, trying to increase the intensity of our contact. I refused to be rushed, slowly running my hand up and down his shaft and thoroughly enjoying his reactions. I flicked my thumb over the head, making sure to caress the tender underside. His breathing quickened when I took his cockhead into my mouth and traced my tongue around it. He tried to push himself deeper, but I held him at bay. At my own pace, I took in a little more of him, focusing the flicks of my tongue on the exquisitely sensitive spot between the head and shaft. I listened to his breathing, and when I heard him gasp, I engulfed his cock until I had taken down most of his veiny length.

A girlfriend once taught me how to deep-throat with a banana, by breathing through my nose and opening up my throat. Now it comes easily for me, and I love having Matthew's whole cock buried deep in my gullet. I rhythmically pressed my tongue against his shaft to tease him, then I eased off but kept his bulbous head inside my mouth. He was breathing faster, so I decided to up the ante. I encircled the base of his shaft with my fingers and sank his cock deep in my throat once again. I coordinated the motions of my hand to follow my lips as they rode up and down his shaft. My warm, wet mouth provided plenty of lubrication for my stroking fist. This maneuver was guaranteed to make him climax.

I kept slamming his cock down my throat and stroking his shaft at the same pace until I felt him shudder. He was obviously fighting hard to keep from coming too soon. His breath quickened, and I felt his pulse pounding in his flesh. I backed off, lightly stroking him with my hand until he calmed down.

Now I began to work a little harder. I alternated between stroking and sucking, deep-throating all I could take. He shuddered each time his cock hit the back of my throat. Matthew loves to watch my lips working his meat. I stared into his eyes as I gorged on him. He began to moan loudly, jacking his hips upward to drive himself into my mouth. I knew he was about to come. Rivulets of sweat began to slip over his skin. I gave him a final teasing suck, and his head popped out of my mouth. I applied pressure to the base of his cock until I felt it stop pulsing.

Matthew was desperate by that point and twined his hands through my hair and began to fuck my face. I moaned loudly around his cock when he was all the way down my throat. He held my head in place to receive his urgent thrusts. His dick felt as if it had doubled in size in my mouth. As he began to pound even more deeply into my throat, my groans urged him on. Finally, his cock began to twitch as he reached the point of no return. Hot come spewed into my mouth as he climaxed. I almost gagged on the amount but managed to swallow it all.

Matthew exhaled, looking like he might collapse onto the floor. A devilish grin soon returned to his lips, and when he finally caught his breath, he looked at me seductively and whispered, "Your turn."

That was a fabulous afternoon, but we had an even better lip-service session just the other night. I'd picked up a bottle of champagne and some strawberries on the way home from work. I walked in to find Matthew in the shower and a roaring fire in the fireplace. I slipped into a silk nightgown and put the bottle of champagne on ice. Matthew came out of the bathroom wearing a plush robe and a roguish grin.

"I thought we were going out tonight," he said as he eyed my sexy gown.

"I thought we'd eat in," I replied seductively, raising one eyebrow as I uncrossed my legs to flash my bare pussy at him.

I'd moved our velvet lounge chairs so that they faced each other. Matthew looked at me hungrily as he sat in the chair opposite mine. I smiled and handed him a champagne flute. I delicately picked up a strawberry and spread my legs, allowing the silken fabric to shift and expose my naked womanhood. His eyes followed my movements as I teased my clit lightly with the strawberry, then rimmed my hole with the tip of it. Matthew was breathless as I brought the fruit up to my mouth. I noticed that he had let his robe fall open, and his exposed cock was temptingly erect.

I told Matthew to play with himself. He dipped his fingers in his champagne and dribbled a little on his cockhead. My mouth started watering. Using the champagne as lubrication, he pumped his stiffening rod a few times. His hand slid gracefully up his shaft, leaving a glistening trail. He flicked his thumb over the head of his cock, then slid his hand back down to his balls, cupping them gently. I hadn't realized what an expert tease my husband could be.

Matthew doubled his efforts, increasing the speed of his hand. I had my fingers on my clit, strumming myself as I watched him. Tiny electric shocks traveled through my body, making me shudder and moan. I surrendered to the sensations and allowed my orgasm to build. Matthew's gaze felt like white-hot light on my body. I could feel his eyes on my throat, breasts, tummy and madly working fingers.

My orgasm crept up quickly. I pumped my fingers into my hole, making wet, smacking sounds. Matthew groaned and licked his lips, keeping his eyes focused on my pussy. My hips began to rock in time with my delving digits. I flicked my thumb against my clit as my fingers filled me, sparking an explosion of bliss that thrilled my entire body.

My hand had moved away from my sex, but the pleasure lingered. Matthew was now between my thighs, his lips wrapped around my clit. He tenderly sucked my pearl, flicking the engorged flesh with his tongue-tip and teasing another gentle orgasm out of me. When he finally came up for air, his lips and chin were glazed with my juice. I kissed him and licked my sweetness off his face. I looked down and saw that his beautiful, neglected cock was ragingly erect and my mouth watered.

I stood and pushed him backward onto the rug in front of the fireplace. The colors of the flames danced warmly on our flesh. I devoured his mouth, kissing him passionately. I traced a line of kisses down his neck and chest to reach his cock. I snuggled between his thighs to enjoy my erotic feast. I nuzzled his balls and moaned in appreciation when I felt his body tense with excitement.

I captured his cock between my lips, and his hard flesh slid smoothly down my throat. Matthew reacted like a wild man. His hands tangled in my hair and held my head in place. His hips began to buck and grind his cock into my mouth. I underestimated how close my man was to orgasm. He was hot and ready. I began to stroke his asshole, and his thrusts grew harder and more intense. Now I could tell he was very close.

I nudged the tip of a spit-slickened finger into the tight ring of his ass. His hips flew upward, and he jammed his cock into my throat. Matthew let out a guttural groan of ecstasy. I concentrated on his pleasure and pushed my finger deeper into his ass. I must have hit some magic button inside him, because he began to climax. His cock virtually exploded into my mouth, gushing salty cream.

Afterward, my husband was completely spent. I curled up against him and watched the flames flickering in the fireplace. Red-hot tongues of fire leaped and danced, reminding me of our hot oral sex and making me daydream of our next lip-service adventure.

Cabin Fever

Peter Berman

We bought the cabin for a song. We hadn't even been looking for a vacation home. I'd been perusing the real-estate section of the local newspaper during brunch one Sunday morning, and an ad for the little fixer-upper by the lake caught my eye. Before long, I was picturing us spending long weekends in the woods—and imagining all of the trouble we could get into with no one around to witness our antics. I easily convinced my wife, Jessica, to go check out the cabin with me.

I loved the place immediately, but there was one thing that gave Jess pause: it was so deep in the woods that there was no connection to electricity, phone lines and—*gasp!*—the Internet. To me that was just another reason to adore the place. Besides, I had a funny feeling that even without access to modern technology, we could find interesting ways to keep ourselves busy.

Of course, I was thinking sexy, already envisioning hours of eating my wife's cunt. And having my dick sucked in return sounded like an appealing prospect—in fact, I was hard simply from imagining some deep-woods oral fun. Seeing the all-too-familiar mischievous look on my face, Jessica softened her anti-cabin stance, and we were soon standing in a broker's office and signing our names on the dotted line.

A few weeks later, we were at our new little hideaway, blowing up an air mattress before changing into bathing suits and running to the lake. Soon I stood in waist-deep water as I watched Jess minnow beneath the surface, her red-bikinied bottom poking up from time to time, and my dick grew hard. I surreptitiously stroked the bulge in my shorts, which I quickly realized weren't necessary. Since there was no one around for miles, I stepped out of the unneeded garment and tossed it onto the shore. The next time my wife swam close, I grabbed at one of the strings that kept her top tied around her neck and tugged it loose. That brought her sputtering up from the deep, giving her the first glimpse of my nudity. A naughty smile played at the corners of her mouth as she cocked an eyebrow and quickly copied me, tossing her top and bottom onto the beach with my trunks. She paddled close and stood up, water streaming from her tits as she wrapped her arms around my neck. We kissed, and my hard-on jabbed her upper thigh as I snaked a hand around to cup one of her asscheeks while tweaking an erect nipple with two fingers of the other hand. She ground her cunt against me in response, and then maneuvered me backward until my cock and balls rose above the water.

Trailing her damp fingers over my arms, Jessica kissed her way down my body until she was on her knees in the wet sand. My prick, streaming precome, twitched when she neared it, but she passed it right by. Instead, she ducked her head beneath my rod, took hold of my asscheeks and began laving my sensitive balls.

Her breasts bobbed in the cool, green water as she took broad swipes along my sac, which drew in at the touch of her tongue. My eyes widened as my gorgeous wife opened her mouth and sucked in one pendulous orb. My body tensed, forcing me to grab her head for support, and then my buttocks clenched as I groaned. I could hardly believe that I was close to coming even though this was the beginning of the blow job; she had yet to go anywhere near my shaft.

Luckily, she didn't make me wait much longer. First, she sucked my other ball until I was moaning uncontrollably, and that noise only got louder when she released my testicles to place a tender kiss on the tip of my cock. She wrapped her lips around my bulbous knob and gave it a good, hard suck. All I could do was stand there, with my fingers threaded through her hair as I gripped her scalp tightly, and prepare for the inevitable oral onslaught.

Her tongue pressed against my crown. Pausing there, she drew rings around the head for a while before sliding her lips along my shaft. My dick twitched against her upper palate as she slowly made her way over my hard-on, and my balls drew inward when her nose neared my still-damp pubic curls. Finally, she was ready for the big event. After swallowing a couple times so that her throat muscles contracted around me, she drew back her head and dragged her tongue along my length.

Digging her fingers into my buttocks, Jessica held on tight as she bobbed her head, and I tried my hardest to stave off the inevitable. I knew I couldn't hold out for long, but I figured I'd do the best I could while I still had control of my senses. Meanwhile, she persisted in pumping me with her mouth, keeping her lips so tight that it felt like I was fucking her hot, wet pussy.

When the vein on the underside of my shaft started throbbing uncontrollably, I imagined the thrill it gave her to feel that pulsing against her tongue. My wife is an expert cocksucker, and what pleases her most is knowing that her efforts are appreciated. And I was about to give her the ultimate tribute: a mouthful of my hot cream.

My body started trembling, warning us both that the end was near, so Jessica picked up her pace. Letting go of one of my asscheeks, she gave my balls a good, hard squeeze, eliciting a grunt from me. As if that weren't enough, she snaked a dainty finger between my buttocks and massaged my asshole. The pressure induced another grunt, which Jess echoed by humming, causing sweet vibrations along my prick. It would take a very strong man to withstand that much stimulation, and since I am not that man, I promptly filled her mouth with my release.

My knees buckled and my body shook as blast after blast of white-hot semen surged from my balls. Almost as soon as I'd eject one salvo, another would follow, but Jessica never flinched. Instead, she swallowed each shot with aplomb, all the while looking up at me with her big, beautiful brown eyes as though imploring me for more. And I gave it to her, my hips rocking back and forth as I shot my load, driving my cock even deeper down her throat.

Eventually, my body stopped convulsing, and the deluge ebbed to a trickle. My grip on her head loosened, and the blood rushed back to my knuckles, turning them from white back to pink. Jessica released her lip-lock, and as my softening prick slid out, I pulled her to her feet. As much as I had enjoyed my orgasm, my favorite part of oral sex was about to occur—returning the favor.

I kissed her on the mouth, sucking the taste of my musk from her tongue. To convey her growing need, she ground herself against me, so I kissed my way down her neck, over her shoulders and to her tits, where I stopped to suckle one extremely ripe nipple.

She writhed as my tongue ringed her crinkled areola, and I heard a moan from above me. Encouraged, I continued my journey down to her stomach, where I flicked at her belly button while inserting my thumb between her dewy labia. I shifted my digit to part the velvety lips, and she opened her legs wider, planting her feet in the loamy sand.

Her cunt splayed, making its delicate insides accessible to my touch and giving me a whiff of her luscious scent. My mouth watered as I breathed in deeply, so I extended my tongue to touch her shimmering pink flesh, which seemed to ripple in expectation. I soon made contact and got my first taste—at least for that day—of my wife's delectable pussy.

She squirmed against my face as I began licking her slick skin. I grabbed her asscheeks to hold her steady, just as she'd done with me, while continuing to lap up the fluids that poured from her hole and dripped down my chin. Her clit was stiff against my tongue, but I was careful not to press too hard, in an attempt to delay her orgasm. Instead, I laved the petals surrounding it, and they quivered at my touch.

Next, I sucked the slippery folds between my lips, and Jessica started gasping and bucking her hips, which mashed her cunt against my teeth. More honey gushed from her opening, and I swallowed it down, loving the rush of fragrant liquid. Craving more of her heavenly nectar, I stiffened my tongue and penetrated her as deeply as I could.

She squealed at my invasion, and ever alert to my wife's needs,

I pulled my tongue out as fast as I'd shoved it in and replaced it with my index finger. Her body lurched as I impaled her on my digit and stroked her from inside. I recommenced licking her tender flesh, still studiously avoiding her throbbing center.

She grabbed my head, and her hold tightened the longer I thrust into her pussy, which was now so wet that my repeated ingress was easy. So easy, in fact, that I finger-fucked her even harder as my tongue darted between her quivering folds. Soon, she was quaking against my face, signaling the onset of her orgasm.

For the grand finale, I moved my tongue to her rigid button and forcefully pressed against her clit. She began shaking violently as I flicked my tongue back and forth. Then she started yelping into the wind, so I tightened my grip on her asscheeks as the lake water churned around us.

As Jessica came, I kept licking her slippery flesh, which quivered against my mouth. Her clit was perfectly stiff, so in an attempt to make her go really crazy, I wrapped my lips around it and gave her a thorough suck. She cried out, and I worked her even harder, teasing her clit with my tongue as I upped the pace of my still-thrusting finger, even though the constrictions of her cunt made that increasingly difficult. She shouted again, louder now, motivating me to lick, suck and finger-fuck her even more forcefully, provoking even more noise. I even chimed in, moaning against my wife's sex to give her the benefit of the vibrations. After all, with no one around us for miles, I knew nobody would hear.

Jessica's body went taut before she gave a heave and slipped from my grasp. Lacking the strength to support her own weight, she joined me on her knees. I wrapped my arms around her waist and held her to me so tightly that her breasts flattened against my chest. We kissed, and she practically inhaled her own essence from my mouth. As the afternoon light turned to dusk, we resumed our swim, overjoyed at being able to cool down in the refreshing water.

From that day on, Jessica was a big fan of the lake house. We soon discovered that no meal is as good as one cooked over a campfire that you've built yourself, and whenever we venture into the woods, we always prepare a celebratory barbecue. We bring a small cooler full of meat, enough to last that initial evening, and I always look forward to seeing my wife wrap her lips around an all-beef hot dog, which never fails to get me hard.

We almost always end our meal with s'mores, sandwiching char-blackened marshmallows and pieces of milky chocolate between squares of graham crackers. One night, while watching Jess lick the residue of the squishy, white confection from her fingertips, I lost interest in my own dessert and tossed my toasting stick onto the flames, my marshmallow still only slightly brûléed. I was hungry for a different sort of treat, so I pulled her hand from her mouth and brought it to my own.

Her face was aglow from the nearby fire as she watched me wrap my lips around one digit to suck off the remains of the sticky sugar. I moved to the next one and sucked it clean as well, and then on to the next, working each candy-coated digit in turn. Even after her whole hand was spotless, I continued running my tongue over her skin and suckling her fingers. In response, she moved her hand to my lap and traced the outline of my erection through my pant leg, and as she stroked, a spot of precome soaked through the denim.

The next thing I knew, she had pulled out my stiff dick and

was pumping it in her fist. As I performed my oral ministrations on her dainty fingers, my appetite grew, until I was starving for a taste of her sweet pussy. I pulled myself from her grasp—albeit somewhat reluctantly, because the feeling of her hand on my cock was divine—and slid off the log we'd been using as a bench.

Kneeling before her, I quickly undid her fly, and she lifted her ass so I could pull off her pants. She sat back down, and I was glad that we'd laid a thick blanket over the log, because it safeguarded her buttocks from the scratchy bark.

As I positioned myself between my wife's thighs, I kept my jeans around my knees to protect them from the leaf-coated ground. Her scent, which now wafted upward, commingled with that of the campfire, creating a craving in me that was almost primal. My own fires now stoked to skyscraping levels, I dove right into her cunt, plastering my lips to her labia and nibbling at the delicate inner folds.

Jessica clutched my shoulders as I gripped her hips, and the sounds of my slurping were intermittently interrupted by a pop or snap from the nearby blaze. I had her writhing within seconds, and she mashed herself against my face. As I trailed my tongue over her fluttering petals, my cock grew harder and my sac started throbbing.

Normally, I try to eat her pussy for as long as possible, prolonging the pleasure for us both, but something told me I wouldn't have that luxury on this occasion. My balls were already dangerously close to bursting, so if I wanted to come somewhere other than on the ground by my knees, I'd have to pick up the pace and get my prick into my wife's pussy pretty damn quick. So I began moving my mouth inward, licking circles around her pulsating button, making them smaller and smaller until I was lashing her clit.

I was expecting an instantaneous explosion, but to my surprise, she pushed me away and stood up. Grabbing the blanket off the log, she spread it on the ground and pulled me onto it with her. Next she straddled my lap, and I could feel her wet heat against my shaft as she leaned forward to press her lips to mine. I assumed that this was a prelude to rising up and impaling herself on my rigid pole, but instead, she spun around and planted her dripping-wet cunt right on my face.

The world went dark, but I didn't mind as I reveled in the feeling of her hot, slick flesh against my mouth. Better yet, she began flicking her tongue over my cockhead, eventually wrapping her lips around my entire knob and sucking.

Unbidden, my hips rose skyward, feeding her even more of my prodigious length. No stranger to this sort of response, Jessica moved with me, sliding her lips to the top of my shaft and then dropping downward when my ass once again hit the blanket. Relaxing her throat as much as possible, she swallowed my dick inch by inch until my pubic curls tickled her nose. She paused with her mouth wrapped around my root, and I could feel the warm, erratic exhalations from her nostrils as she waited until she was certain I'd regained some semblance of control. Only then did she commence rising and falling on my sturdy erection, all the while swishing her tempting tongue back and forth across the topside of my shaft.

My wife's juices poured onto my face as she bobbed over my pole, swallowing it repeatedly. In return, my tongue thrashed her pussy, stimulating her silky flesh as I vacuumed up her free-flowing honey. Her throat muscles tightened around me, so I increased my assault, nipping gently at her interior labia before moving to her clit.

Just as I did that, Jessica grabbed my balls and squeezed them tight. My creamy come started percolating as she massaged my sac, and more precome trickled from the slit in my crown. As she moaned her appreciation, her throat muscles vibrated, sending chills down my spine. I reciprocated by groaning against her pussy as I pulled at her clit with my lips, suddenly desperate to get her off. My own impending orgasm was driving me, as well as the hope that we'd arrive at our pinnacles together.

Reaching up, I slid a finger into her entryway and began thrusting in and out. She rewarded me with a mouthful of juices, so I stroked harder, anxious to aid her in reaching her goal. Her cunt contracted around my digit, and a second later, my entire shaft was deep in her throat.

Meanwhile, she mewled through her own climax, her thighs clamped tightly against my head to offset the tremors wracking her body. Her cunt mashed against my mouth, and I kept sucking her pulsating clitoris to keep the quaking going, though I stopped plunging my finger in and out of her. Instead, I kept it buried deep inside, trying to locate the spot along her canal that makes her go seriously wild.

I knew I'd found the right location when her entire body went tense. Ripping her mouth off my cock, she shrieked into the star-filled sky as my load spurted upward like a geyser. Though I couldn't see it, I could picture the pearly white liquid spattering across her tits, which made me come even harder. My shaft throbbed as cream coated my stomach and pooled in my patch of wiry curls, and Jess joined in the fun by feeding me another mouthful of her essence. Finally, my balls were depleted and Jessica's pussy grew ultrasensitive, so she turned back around until we were once again face-to-face.

We kissed, and I marveled at the effect that buying the cabin had had on our sex life. Maybe it was the freedom of getting away from the busy, bustling city, or merely just the fresh, pine-tinged air, but something about being out in nature had really gotten our motors running. And with miles and miles of woods around us, the possibilities for future oral adventures were endless.

Late-Night Snack

Mike Schwimmer

The last thing I want to think about after a hard night at work is cooking. Why? Because I run a kitchen at a small, busy restaurant in the city—and I'm slammed from about 6:00 p.m. until 11:00 p.m. What *do* I want? To peel off my whites, sit in an empty corner booth and watch the fish swim in the tank. God, do I love those fucking fish. There's something mesmerizing about the way they seem to dance—the delicate fins fluttering, the iridescent colors gleaming under the bright lights.

This is exactly what I was doing when I suddenly spotted something—well—fishy.

I'll admit that my first reaction was complete surprise. I had thought the place was closed. In fact, I'd closed it myself. I set my scotch on the table and moved closer to inspect. When I got in front of the tank, I saw a perfect torso, beautiful breasts and long curly red hair. Was there a mermaid in our fish tank? No, it was Jasmine, the lovely hostess who spends her nights making sure our customers are enjoying their meals to the fullest.

But now she was standing behind our fish tank naked, and I felt like a cartoon character, my jaw literally dropping toward my chest. We'd been flirting for a few months now, but I had never made a move. Why? Mostly because by the end of my shift, I'm too tired to move much of anything.

For a moment, I worried. Should I offer her a drink? Pull up a chair? Get her a robe? Then I realized she was the one who had set this up. Maybe she had plans.

She sure was lovely. I stared through the tank at her. My cock stirred in the loose black-and-white pants I had on. Maybe I wasn't so tired after all.

Jasmine came around the tank carrying a bottle of champagne and two glasses. "I would have brought wine," she said with a sly smile, "but I didn't know where I could carry the corkscrew."

I laughed. My favorite thing about her so far—even more than her knockout body—was her sense of humor. She always had a positive spin on a situation, which came in handy when there was any foul-up at the restaurant, such as a missing reservation or a meal gone awry. Jasmine had a light touch. I watched as she set down the bottle and the glasses, and I sat back down in my booth.

"You look amazing," I said. I couldn't get over the fact that she was naked.

"This old thing?" She spun around, so I could see her slim body from all angles. "I've had it for years."

I stared at her pert, athletic build, drinking her in. She had a small tattoo above her hip—a mermaid with a turquoise tail. I smiled. "What made you decide to take off your clothes?"

"I've always found that it's easier to fuck without them."

Had my cock stirred before? It was at full mast now. "So we're fucking?"

"No, Mike. We're talking. But in a minute, we'll be fucking."

Christ. Those were all the hints I needed. I stood up again and grabbed her around the waist, then lifted her onto the table. Why should she have all the fun?

"What are you doing, Mike?" She widened her huge blue eyes at me.

"I'm hungry," I said. "I didn't get a chance to catch a bite."

"So catch…"

She lay down on the table. I moved my scotch, the champagne and the glasses onto the table next to ours, and then I sat back down in the U-shaped part of the booth and parted her thighs. The first thing I noticed was that she was shaved. I liked that. I'd wondered—during those casual, carnal moments when you wrap your hand around your cock and wonder about your hot hostess—whether she'd have a full bush, a landing strip or be completely bare. Jasmine was shaved nude, her skin smooth and soft. I pulled her closer to me and bent to lick her pussy for the first time, savoring the way her slick juices teased my tongue.

Even though I felt as if I'd fallen headfirst into ambrosia, Jasmine was the one who sighed. I felt that sigh reverberate through me. Her taste was delicious. Sometimes—some lucky times—you connect with a lover who fits perfectly with you. Jasmine tasted like the definition of freshness. I wanted to eat her for hours. From the purring sounds of pleasure she was making, I got the feeling she wouldn't have minded a bit. Slowly, I parted her pussy lips with my fingers and then I began to make spirals with my tongue around her clit. Eating out a woman is something I truly adore. Maybe it's because I like to be in charge. I know how to run a kitchen—and I know how to give a woman pleasure. But I also have a refined palate. Dining on a sweet-tasting pussy is one of the greatest pleasures in my life.

I worked her slowly, steadily, with the same attention to detail I give every dish on my menu. I pressed my face to the split of her body, then moved my head back and forth. I could tell that she liked the way my long hair felt against her thighs. Her whole body jumped, as if electrified, then slowly settled back again. I waited for a moment, and then I licked her clit firmly with the tip of my tongue. She groaned and I arched. I loved the way she moved. She was reactive to every touch. Finally, when I could stand to wait no longer, I sucked her clit forcefully between my lips, giving her a tiny glimmer of what was to come.

"Oh yes," she whimpered sexily. "Mike, that feels so fucking good."

I have always liked it when a girl says my name while we're making love. And I have always been a fan of girls who swear. I don't know why. There's just something raw about the way a girl says, "fuck." Jasmine hit the word exactly right. The fact that I'd only heard her behave in a refined manner up until now was simply icing.

Part of me wanted to hurry. I knew that I could get her off if I worked her just right. But I also wanted to savor the moment. Jasmine's delicate flavor was so sweet, her juices so abundant and creamy.

I didn't want the hors d'oeuvres to be over too soon.

I kept licking, and she kept sighing, wiggling her hips a little on the cool tabletop when I hit the right spot. We moved in a perfect rhythm. I knew we'd actually fuck before the night was over, but I was determined to get her off once, a good solid orgasm, before we went any further. She deserved a reward, didn't she? She'd taken that first brave step, made the first bold move. And rather than simply appear with champagne, she'd appeared like a mermaid, a vision, hair long and loose down her pale skin, body all ripe and ready.

"Get this wet for me," I said, leaning forward so she could lick my fingers.

"Why?"

"I'm going to finger-fuck your pussy while I suck your clit."

She shivered and I smiled. How many times had I already fucked her—in my mind, that is? Too many to count. Ever since she'd been hired, I had imagined what she'd feel like on my cock, what she'd taste like under my tongue. I'd had her in the coat-check room, back by the bathrooms, bent over the butcher block, at the main dais. All in my head. Now that fantasy had become sweet reality, I realized that my imagination had never done the job properly. This girl was so hot, so sexy. Every jerk-off session I'd had fizzled in comparison to what she really tasted like, felt like, sounded like.

I watched as Jasmine parted her cherry-glossed lips and then began to lick my fingers slowly, and my cock got even harder, although I wouldn't have thought that was possible. What's harder than rock? What's harder than titanium? I felt as if I had a steel rod inside my chef pants. Her mouth on my fingers let me know exactly what it would feel like when she wrapped her lips around my rod.

"Make me come, Mike," Jasmine begged when she let my fingers slip free.

"Is that an order?"

"A special request."

"I'll see if the kitchen is up to it."

I sat back down and began to lick her pussy once more. But as I suckled on her clit, I slowly slid two fingers up inside her, one crossed over the other. She tightened on me. I sighed, daydreaming about what her snug pussy would feel like around my cock. As soon as I had that thought, Jasmine said, "This is even better."

"Better?"

"Than what I fantasized."

So she'd shared the same dirty thoughts I had.

"Since I first saw you..." She was panting now. "All I could think about was figuring out how to get you to fuck me."

We had waited months. We could have been doing this from the get-go.

"I love the way you look when you cook, so serious. Your hair back in the ponytail. Your whole attitude one of 'don't fuck with me now.' That's all I've wanted to do. Fuck you."

I felt a slight sadness over all those make-out and make-love sessions we'd missed. But then I became determined to make this one so outstanding we'd never look back. I kept working my fingers up in her, working my tongue on her pearl, until I felt her reach that place where she was teetering on the brink. Right then, I stood up and moved to the head of the table. She helped me by sliding her body around so that her pussy was right on the edge. I lowered my slacks and slammed my cock inside her, and she gasped and stared at me.

"You're going to come on my cock," I told her.

"And then I'm going to lick all the juices off," she said, finishing the thought.

Who was this girl? She was like the other half of me. Everything I thought, she had already worked out. I held her hips and pounded into her. I let one of my hands slide between us so that I could keep touching her clit while we fucked. When she leaned her head back, her hair all spirals of cinnamon around her, I knew she was coming. Yeah, I could have let go and come with her, but I didn't want to. Not yet. Not with what she had promised hanging out there between us. I made sure she got every last ounce of pleasure she had coming to her. And then I watched—me with the wide eyes this time—as she urged me back and spun around once more. She was naked, and glistening.

Oh yeah, and she was hungry...

While I watched, she opened her full lips once more and took my cock inside her mouth. I don't know that I've ever seen anything that beautiful before. Her mouth was slicked with that cherry lipstick, and in seconds the lipstick had smeared on my rod. I groaned and pushed forward, but she backed away.

"You let me do it," she said, and I bit my lip and steeled myself. This was her night. Another time, I could set the pace. But she had gone to all this trouble for me. I ought to let her do what she wanted. Especially, since what she wanted seemed to be to give me the best blow job of my fucking life.

While I clenched my hands into fists at my sides, she bobbed up and down on my cock. I could feel the pleasure building inside me, the pressure in my balls, the desire in my belly. She was working me with such finesse that I realized I was holding my breath. I exhaled hard and sucked in a breath again. I'd never had to remind myself to breathe before. But the pleasure was so intense that my brain seemed incapable of ordering my body to do even the most basic commands. I inhaled and exhaled, and Jasmine swallowed more and more of my cock down her throat.

Suddenly, I realized I didn't have to be immobile. I could touch her. Slowly, I stroked her long red hair, let my fingers caress her naked skin, let my hands wander over her body. Jasmine moaned when I touched her, and I felt that moan on my cock. The girl was good. She knew exactly what to do. At least, I thought she did. Because before I could figure out what was happening, she was in motion.

Wait, I wanted to say. *I'm not done yet. I'm close, but I'm not done.*

And then I saw what she was doing.

She maneuvered herself so that she was on her back, head hanging over the table, mouth open at cock level. Damn, she looked sexy.

"Fuck me, Mike," she said. "Fuck my mouth."

Oh, holy shit. I couldn't believe the words that had just left her lips. Slowly, I slid my cock into her. She tightened her mouth around my rod. I moved back and forth. She kept with the rhythm. While I watched, she started to play with herself. She was sucking me off and trailing her long, delicate fingers over her pussy. Jesus. I kept moving, my hips shifting back and forth, fucking her sweet, warm mouth as long as I could manage. Then I had to be inside her again. I pulled away, and she reached for me.

But I was done with her setting the stage. I'd lied about giving her free rein. Now I needed to be in charge. I grabbed her and carried her to the longest table in the dining room. Thank god it hadn't been reset yet for the following night's service. If it had, I would have simply knocked all of the dishes onto the floor. I was in need. Badly. I set her down on the table and stared at her. Her skin was pale and luminous, her pussy wet and ready. I stripped out of my clothes faster than I ever had before, and then I turned toward the table, prepared to climb on top, but Jessie stopped me.

"Wait, Mike. Come closer and turn around again."

I stepped forward and then showed her my back. She started laughing. "You've got a mermaid, too." She'd spotted the tattoo on my lower back. I felt her fingertips tracing over the design. But I couldn't take the time to discuss coincidences right now.

"I have to be in you again."

"Yes, Mike."

"I've gotta fuck you."

"Yes."

I climbed onto the table and positioned myself over her lithe body. She stared into my eyes as I pressed the head of my cock at her entrance. She was wetter than I'd ever felt a woman before. I wondered what was turning her on the most. For me, it was all the waiting we'd done. This was the culmination of months of flirtatious foreplay. But it was more than that. I felt a connection to her. Something strong and powerful. She seemed to know exactly what I was thinking, what I was wanting, almost before I did.

Like now. She wrapped one of her hands around my shaft and directed me inside her. Her warm fist wrapped around my rod, followed by her warmer, wetter pussy around my cock. I locked eyes with her and pushed forward into heaven. She let me drive inside her slippery-wet canal, and then her thighs came around and she held me to her. That felt so amazing—to be embraced by her strong legs as I fucked her hard. The whole table shook with the power of our love-making.

"When you come," she said, "I want to suck you again." She trailed her long fingernails down my back as she spoke. A shiver ran through me—both from her words and from her actions.

"I want to taste your juices mixed with mine. Because we're sweet together."

Jesus, the girl was dirty. I like that in a lover.

"I want to make you all hard again, so you can fuck me up against the fish tank. The cool glass against my back. I can already feel it."

"Oh yeah."

"We don't have anywhere to go. We can be here all night. We can fuck all night long."

I couldn't speak. I think I nodded. Mostly, I just slammed against her. Her body fit mine like we were made for each other. I drove my cock inside her, and the muscles in her pussy tightened and released. I ground my hips against her, and she moaned and raised her body to meet mine. We were rocking together forcefully, and I was grateful that our tables are sturdy—nothing flimsy to buckle beneath us. Because she was bringing out a nearly animalistic side of myself that had until that moment been hidden. It was sensual and nearly overwhelming.

Right when I got close to the edge, she moved us so that I was on my back and she was astride me. Her long red hair flickered around her as she fucked me. I loved this new view. I reached up and stroked her pert breasts, ran my thumbs over her hard nipples. She bit her lip and flexed her thighs, rocking herself on my cock. She looked so pretty like that, and I wished I could have taken the time to truly admire her—but honestly, at that point, all I could think about was coming.

"You fill me up," she whispered. "I can feel you all the way through me."

I bucked, raising her up into the air.

"Don't forget," she said, "I want to go down on you again as soon as you come."

And then all I could think about was the fact that she wanted to suck me clean. We would sixty-nine. I could see that in my mind. We'd get each other all wet and slippery once more before starting over. I couldn't decide which I wanted more—to be in her pussy or in her mouth, to be staring up at her the way I was now, or to be face-to-cunt with her sweet snatch. I still had her flavor on my tongue. I never wanted to taste anything else.

She started to ride me even harder, and I groaned, "I'm there."

"Come for me, baby," she said, "because I'm coming, too."

Sweet relief washed over me. All I had wanted was to reach the end with her—but then, when I looked into her ocean-blue eyes, I realized that maybe there would be no end. And that was fine with me. We were starring in a fish tale in which the fisherman catches the fish—or in this case, a mermaid.

The one who didn't get away.

Welcome to **Life On Top!**

Penthouse, Penthouse Letters, Penthouse Forum and Penthouse Variations offer you all the excitement you can handle. Available monthly at newsstands and bookstores, or call **1-800-455-2392** for your subscription to the hottest magazines available. You can also go to **PenthouseMagazine.com** to order all of your favorites in print and digital formats.

While you're at it, take things up a notch and visit **PenthouseStore.com** for jewelry, lingerie, DVDs and more to spice up your days and nights.

More from Alison Tyler

Frenzy
60 Stories of Sudden Sex
Edited by Alison Tyler

"Toss out the roses and box of candies. This isn't a prolonged seduction. This is slammed against the wall in an alleyway sex, and it's all that much hotter for it."
—Erotica Readers & Writers Association
ISBN 978-1-57344-331-9 $14.95

Best Bondage Erotica
Edited by Alison Tyler

Always playful and dangerously explicit, these arresting fantasies grab you, tie you down, and never let you go.
ISBN 978-1-57344-173-5 $15.95

Afternoon Delight
Erotica for Couples
Edited by Alison Tyler

"Alison Tyler evokes a world of heady sensuality where fantasies are fearlessly explored and dreams gloriously realized."
—Barbara Pizio, Executive Editor,
Penthouse Variations
ISBN 978-1-57344-341-8 $14.95

Got a Minute?
60 Second Erotica
Edited by Alison Tyler

"Classy but very, very dirty, this is one of the few very truly indispensable filth anthologies around." —*UK Forum*
ISBN 978-1-57344-404-0 $14.95

Playing with Fire
Taboo Erotica
Edited by Alison Tyler

"Alison Tyler has managed to find the best stories from the best authors, and create a book of fantasies that—if you're lucky enough, or determined enough—just might come true." —Clean Sheets
ISBN 978-1-57344-348-7 $14.95

Happy Endings Forever and Ever

Dark Secret Love
A Story of Submission
By Alison Tyler

Inspired by her own BDSM exploits and private diaries, Alison Tyler draws on twenty-five years of penning sultry stories to create a scorchingly hot work of fiction, a memoir-inspired novel with reality at its core. A modern-day *Story of O*, a *9 1/2 Weeks*-style journey fueled by lust, longing and the search for true love.
ISBN 978-1-57344-956-4 $16.95

High-Octane Heroes
Erotic Romance for Women
Edited by Delilah Devlin

One glance and your heart will melt—these chiseled, brave men will ignite your fantasies with their courage and charisma. Award-winning romance writer Delilah Devlin has gathered stories of hunky, red-blooded guys who enter danger zones in the name of duty, honor, country and even love.
ISBN 978-1-57344-969-4 $15.95

Duty and Desire
Military Erotic Romance
Edited by Kristina Wright

The only thing stronger than the call of duty is the call of desire. *Duty and Desire* enlists a team of hot-blooded men and women from every branch of the military who serve their country and follow their hearts.
ISBN 978-1-57344-823-9 $15.95

Smokin' Hot Firemen
Erotic Romance Stories for Women
Edited by Delilah Devlin

Delilah delivers tales of these courageous men breaking down doors to steal readers' hearts! *Smokin' Hot Firemen* imagines the romantic possibilities of being held against a massively muscled chest by a man whose mission is to save lives and serve *every* need.
ISBN 978-1-57344-934-2 $15.95

Only You
Erotic Romance for Women
Edited by Rachel Kramer Bussel

Only You is full of tenderness, raw passion, love, longing and the many emotions that kindle true romance. The couples in *Only You* test the boundaries of their love to make their relationships stronger.
ISBN 978-1-57344-909-0 $15.95

Many More Than Fifty Shades of Erotica

Try This at Home!

Morning, Noon and Night
Erotica for Couples
Edited by Alison Tyler

Alison Tyler thinks about sex twenty-four hours a day, and the result is *Morning, Noon and Night*, a sizzling collection of headily sensual stories featuring couples whose love fuels their lust. From delicious trysts at dawn to naughty nooners, afternoon delights and all-night-long lovemaking sessions, Alison Tyler is your guide to sultry, slippery sex.
ISBN 978-1-57344-821-5 $15.95

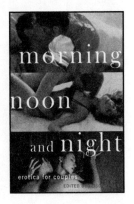

Anything for You
Erotica for Kinky Couples
Edited by Rachel Kramer Bussel

Whether you are a BDSM aficionado or a novice newly discovering the joys of tying up your lover, *Anything for You* will unravel a world of obsessive passion, the kind that lies just beneath the skin.
ISBN 978-1-57344-813-0 $15.95

Sweet Danger
Erotic Stories of Forbidden Desire for Couples
Edited by Violet Blue

Sweet Danger will inspire you with stories of a sexy video shoot, a rough-trade gang bang, a public sex romp served with a side of exquisite humiliation and much, much more. What is *your* deepest, most sweetly dangerous fantasy?
ISBN 978-1-57344-648-8 $14.95

Irresistible
Erotic Romance for Couples
Edited by Rachel Kramer Bussel

Irresistible features loving couples who turn their deepest fantasies into reality—resulting in uninhibited, imaginative sex they can only enjoy together.
ISBN 978-1-57344-762-1 $14.95

Sweet Confessions
Erotic Fantasies for Couples
Edited by Violet Blue

In *Sweet Confessions*, Violet Blue showcases inspirational "you can do it, too" tales that are perfect bedtime reading for lovers. The lust-inciting fantasies include spanking, exhibitionism, role-playing, three-ways and sensual adventures that will embolden real couples to reach new heights of passion.
ISBN 978-1-57344-665-5 $14.95

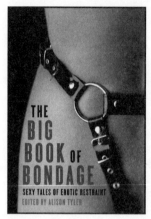

Bestselling Erotica for Couples

Sweet Life
Erotic Fantasies for Couples
Edited by Violet Blue

Your ticket to a front row seat for first-time spankings, breathtaking role-playing scenes, sex parties, women who strap it on and men who love to take it, not to mention threesomes of every combination.
ISBN 978-1-57344-133-9 $14.95

Sweet Life 2
Erotic Fantasies for Couples
Edited by Violet Blue

"This is a we-did-it-you-can-too anthology of real couples playing out their fantasies." —Lou Paget, author of *365 Days of Sensational Sex*
ISBN 978-1-57344-167-4 $15.95

Sweet Love
Erotic Fantasies for Couples
Edited by Violet Blue

"If you ever get a chance to try out your number-one fantasies in real life—and I assure you, there will be more than one—say yes. It's well worth it. May this book, its adventurous authors, and the daring and satisfied characters be your guiding inspiration."—Violet Blue
ISBN 978-1-57344-381-4 $14.95

Afternoon Delight
Erotica for Couples
Edited by Alison Tyler

"Alison Tyler evokes a world of heady sensuality where fantasies are fearlessly explored and dreams gloriously realized."
—Barbara Pizio, Executive Editor, *Penthouse Variations*
ISBN 978-1-57344-341-8 $14.95

Three-Way
Erotic Stories
Edited by Alison Tyler

"Three means more of everything. Maybe I'm greedy, but when it comes to sex, I like more. More fingers. More tongues. More limbs. More tangling and wrestling on the mattress." —from the introduction
ISBN 978-1-57344-193-3 $15.95

Ordering is easy! Call us toll free or fax us to place your MC/VISA order.
You can also mail the order form below with payment to:
Cleis Press, 2246 Sixth St., Berkeley, CA 94710.

ORDER FORM

QTY	TITLE	PRICE
———	———————————————————————	———————
———	———————————————————————	———————
———	———————————————————————	———————
———	———————————————————————	———————
———	———————————————————————	———————
———	———————————————————————	———————
———	———————————————————————	———————
———	———————————————————————	———————

SUBTOTAL   _____

SHIPPING   _____

SALES TAX   _____

TOTAL   _____

Add $3.95 postage/handling for the first book ordered and $1.00 for each additional book. Outside North America, please contact us for shipping rates. California residents add 9% sales tax. Payment in U.S. dollars only.

* Free book of equal or lesser value. Shipping and applicable sales tax extra.

Cleis Press • Phone: (800) 780-2279 • Fax: (510) 845-8001
orders@cleispress.com • www.cleispress.com
You'll find more great books on our website

Follow us on Twitter @cleispress • Friend/fan us on Facebook